THE Wizard OF PRIDE

Ryan Field

The Wizard of Pride© 2021 Ryan Field

For more information contact:
Riverdale Avenue Books/Magnus Imprint
5676 Riverdale Avenue
Riverdale, NY 10471
www.riverdaleavebooks.com

Design by www.formatting4U.com
Cover design by Scott Carpenter

Digital ISBN: 9781626015876
Trade ISBN: 9781626015883

First edition, June 2021

Author's Note

The *Wizard of Oz* has remained a classic story for years, and it certainly will remain that way for many years to come. However, as with all classics stories from the past, LGBTQ+ people were invisible at best and comic relief at worst. Of course this doesn't take anything away from *The Wizard of Oz*, and it doesn't make the story any better or worse. It's simply a fact that can't be disputed, and society has reached a point where it can at least be recognized as a fact.

With that said, *The Wizard of Pride* isn't paying homage to *The Wizard of Oz,* and it's not laughing at it either. It's simply a parody, with a certain amount of good-natured sarcasm, and it's a work of fiction that suggests what might have happened if Dorothy had been a young gay man named Darius who woke up and found himself in a place called *The Land of Pride* instead of *The Land of Oz*. It's more of a tongue-in-cheek account with references to gay culture and realities we know nowadays that weren't even conceived in the year 1939, when the film was made. For example, the main character, Darius, lands in a place called *Pride*, he meets a beautiful fairy princess who's really a man in drag, and he sets off to find *The Wonderful Wizard of Pride* who lives in a place called *The Rainbow City*, where all people are equal and no one is judged for being LGBTQ+. Of course there's a love story and there is erotic escapades, however, it's also a celebration of all the achievements that have become realities for LGBTQ people since the original *Wizard of Oz* was first introduced to the world. And most of all, it's total fantasy that never would have been published anywhere in 1939.

Even though the trope is still the same, the characters, the dialogue, and the situations aren't the same because they're all geared toward gay culture and what it's like to always be living on the outside looking in. At times it's campy and at times it's serious, but there's always that underlying message of the need to feel love and to be accepted.

I do hope you will enjoy this re-imaging.

Ryan Field, Pride 2021

Chapter One

On late summer afternoons, Darius Krasner would meet one of his secret male friends in the old abandoned barn out at the Riggleby Farm. These guys were farm hands, all young men he'd known for a long time. The Riggleby Farm hadn't been occupied since the late 1920s and it was the safest place for Darius and his secret friends to gather. Darius lived on another farm on the outskirts of a small town in Kansas named Uranus, and in that rural setting it wasn't easy to be himself. For fear of shame, ridicule, and judgment, Darius lived a quiet life and never took chances with his reputation in Uranus. And even though he was only 22 years old, he'd learned the meaning of the word discretion the first time he saw a pair of pink high heels.

One quiet dusty afternoon in August 1939, Darius and his secret friend, Jasper Evans, were rolling around naked on a red plaid blanket at the back of the old barn at the Riggleby Farm when Darius heard a noise. At first he thought it was a rodent, or maybe even a bird. It sounded as if something had knocked into a loose board and there could have been any number of explanations, so he dismissed it completely as insignificant. No one knew they were there. He was too busy at the moment to care, and he rolled over on his back and spread his legs so Jasper could climb on top of him. Darius had two other special friends he met at the barn, but Jasper was his favorite. He was tall, with dark wavy hair, and lanky. His hands were the size of dinner plates and his penis was even more impressive. He would have been perfect if only he'd been able to overcome his insecurities. As handsome and kind as Jasper was, the slightest thing could set him to stammering.

As Darius spread his legs wider, he reached for Jasper's shoulders with both hands and Jasper entered him slowly. Jasper slid in deeper and Darius heard another noise, and this time the noise was followed by a sudden gasp and a piercing scream.

Jasper stopped moving, but he was still deep inside Darius' body. They both looked up at the same time and Darius saw Agnes McCain standing over them. She had her palms pressed to her flat skinny chest, her eyes wide, and her pinched pie hole of a mouth was wide open. She glared at them and said, "I knew it. I knew you were up to no good in here the minute I saw you two perverts sneaking around this farm a few weeks ago, Darius. And look at you, Jasper Evans. I'm sure your daddy is going to love hearing *this* story."

Jasper pulled out of Darius fast. He jumped up from the old red plaid blanket so he could find his pants and he left Darius flat on his back, naked with his legs still spread. As he reached for his pants, Agnes McCain took one look at his erection, she lost her balance, and she fell back against the wooden support beam.

While Jasper pulled up his pants and looked around for the rest of his clothes, Darius got up from the blanket, pulled some hay out of his hair, and grabbed his pants. He'd left them dangling on a hook near a rusty old shovel. He'd forgotten where he'd left his underpants and he didn't waste time looking for them.

"Oh my God," Jasper said. "I can't believe this happened. What are we going to do? My daddy will kill us both for this." He was stuttering so much it was hard to make out what he was saying.

Darius pulled up his zipper and said, "Calm down, Jasper. Everything will be okay. There's nothing to worry about. You're fine, so just take a deep breath." He knew Jasper only stuttered this way when he was extremely nervous about something.

Agnes McCain stood up straight again and squared her back. "Oh yes, there is something to worry about, you sinners. I'm going to expose you two sinners to this entire town, and then to the entire county, and you're both going to have to repent for the sins you've committed here."

"Oh my God," Jasper said, again. His face was red, his entire body was trembling, and there were beads of sweat dripping down the sides of his face.

Darius already knew about poor Jasper's fears and issues and he didn't want to make things any worse, so he reached out to Agnes and started to beg. "Please, Agnes. Don't tell anyone. Oh please, don't tell. No one else has to know about this. I'll do anything you want. I'll work for free for you. Anything. You just name it. But don't tell anyone about what you just saw."

"Oh no, Darius," she said. "I've seen *you* sneaking in here with those other two boys, too. I've been watching you very closely, Darius. Last week I saw you and Eddie Franklin slip in here when you thought no one was watching, and then a few days ago, while everyone else was at church on Sunday, I saw you

3

sneak in again with Tommy Petersen. I couldn't figure it out at first, but now I know what you do in here. Just how many other guys have you been sneaking around with in here, that's what I'd like to know?"

Jasper stopped and gaped in Darius' direction. "You've been meeting Eddie and Tommy in here, too. Well I didn't know *that*." He was so nervous he continued to stutter. In fact, on a good day when he wasn't stressed at all he often stuttered. "I thought I was the only one you met up with in here."

Agnes McCain laughed. "Apparently, Darius likes to take care of all the young men he knows."

Darius wasn't officially in a relationship with anyone and he'd never felt the need to explain himself to the men he fooled around with on the sly. He had to be discreet for obvious reasons. Jasper, Eddie and Tommy all worked on his family's farm and he'd been fooling around with them, individually, for years. He shifted his gaze to Tommy and shrugged. "I didn't think you'd mind. After all, you're engaged to be married to the Laughlin girl and I never said anything about that. I never expected anything from you. I don't owe anyone any explanations."

"Degenerates, that's what you are," Agnes said. "You're all a bunch of sick perverts and I'm going to expose you all."

At that point Jasper's hands started to shake again. He turned and started running. Darius tried to call after him but he didn't stop. Jasper ran out of the barn and down the dirt road without giving either of them as much as a backward glance.

Darius turned to face Agnes. "Look what you've done to him. Please don't say anything. Please, please don't ruin our lives. If this kind of thing were to get out we would all be ruined, and so would our families."

In one of her more dramatic moves, Agnes lifted her right arm and started to shout the worst pejoratives about men like Darius. The words faggot, queer, homo, and fairy spewed from her twisted old mouth. They were sharp and they cut to his very core, and she shamed him beyond anything he'd ever known. Her wrecked voice reached such a painful level of shrillness that Darius' dog jumped out from behind a rusty old tractor and locked his jaw around Agnes' left arm. Darius knew that Sparky wasn't going to bite her, or harm her. He was simply tugging at her arm to get her to stop screaming at Darius.

Agnes froze and said, "Get this vicious beast off of me or I'll have him put down."

Darius had found Sparky on the side of the road a few years earlier, thin as a spike and so weak he could barely stand up. He'd been abandoned and left to die alone. As far as Darius could tell, he was an American Pit Bull, black and white with more white than black. He was also the calmest, quietest dog Darius had ever encountered and didn't have a hint of meanness in his entire body. Darius' aunt always laughed and said Sparky was the kind of dog on which field mice would rest because they knew they were safe. However, Darius also knew that Agnes despised all dogs and cats and she was known to scour the county looking for strays that she could put down. She'd even been pushing the town council in Uranus to appoint her the official dog catcher.

"He won't hurt you," Darius said. "He's just trying to make you stop screaming."

She screamed even louder. "Get this beast off me, Darius. You know how I feel about dogs."

Darius was fully clothed by then so he went over to where she was standing and tugged on Sparky's collar. He glanced down at Sparky, as if Sparky could understand every word he spoke, and said, "That's enough. I'm fine. Let go of her."

Sparky released her arm, looked up at Darius, and barked. Darius rubbed his head and said, "Good boy. It's okay now. You didn't do anything wrong."

Agnes shook her arm and said, "Oh no it's *not* okay, Darius Krasner. That vicious beast attacked me. He tried to kill me. After I tell Etienne and Nicola what he did, I'm going to tell them what I saw you doing this afternoon with that Evans boy, not to mention the fact that you're trespassing on my property. I'll tell them about the other men, too, and about everything."

Darius shot her a look. "This isn't your property yet, Agnes. You know that Etienne and Nicola have been trying to purchase it for years." Etienne and Nicola were Darius' aunt and uncle and they'd been the people who'd raised him from the time he was an infant. After his mom and dad died in a tornado that tore the entire county apart, Etienne and Nicola took him in as if he was their own. Even though he referred to them in a casual way as Etienne and Nicola, he thought of them as his mom and dad and there was nothing he wouldn't do for them.

Agnes lifted her chin and said, "Well I just came up with the money, a cash deal, and it's going to be my property very soon and there's nothing you can do about that." Agnes was the only real estate agent in

Uranus and she already owned more than half the town. Although she sat in the front row at church on Sunday, and she sang holy songs the loudest, she'd been known to evict families from their homes for missing one rent payment, closing down businesses for missing a mortgage payment, and evicting senior citizens who couldn't even afford their medications. She had the most notorious reputation in the county for being ruthless and most people were terrified of her. If Agnes set out to ruin someone, she usually succeeded. Of course there had been rumors about crooked deals she'd made, and situations that suggested she'd done criminal acts in real estate, but no one could ever prove anything and she knew that.

She was also peculiar and eccentric. She wore black dresses and tailored black waistcoats that she'd had since the Edwardian era, she never wore make up or jewelry, her black hair was always pulled back in a tight little bun, and her nose resembled a parrot's beak. As she turned to climb onto to her bicycle she sent Darius a glance and said, "When I'm finished with you people I'll not only own this farm, I'll own your farm, too. I'll run you and your people out of this county."

"Please don't say anything about what you saw today," Darius said. He squared his back and looked her in the eye. "I swear on my life I will do anything you want. I'll work as hard as I can for you and never charge you a nickel. If you say anything about what you saw you'll be ruining so many lives you'll never be able to live with yourself."

"Oh I'll be able to live with myself because I have morals and good old-fashioned religion on my side. You're the pervert. You're the one who's been seducing those other young men. They all have girlfriends and you're the only one who doesn't. I've heard about your kind before, Darius. And you'll repent for this if it's the last thing I do."

This was true. Jasper, Eddie, and Tommy were all in relationships with local young women and Darius was the only one who'd never even dated women. He couldn't help it if he wasn't wired the same way they were. He'd never been able to fake his feelings. The other guys had been able to find a way to date women and rationalize their attraction to Darius at the same time. And Darius had never asked for anything emotional from them. His relationship with each one of them had been nothing more than physical and he'd never expected more from them. He'd always been very pragmatic that way and he'd learned to live without love or romance in his life. He'd learned to settle for occasional affection, with a man on top of him in a dusty old barn. In 1939, men like Darius didn't have the same chances or opportunities that men who were attracted to women had. As long as he was discreet and minded his own business, no one ever asked any questions. He also suspected he wasn't the only so-called bachelor living in a small rural town in the middle of America.

As Agnes peddled away from him, he called after her and said, "What can I do? There must be something I can do to make you rethink exposing all of us this way. You're right. I'm the one to blame, not the other guys. Just tell me what you want."

She stopped peddling and turned to glance back at him with a wicked expression. "I want that beast of a dog put down, and then maybe I'll think about keeping our little secret, at least for the time being. And on top of that, I won't say anything about the other men you've been sinning with. I'll leave them out of this out of respect for their families. But you will owe me, and it starts with that beast of a dog. It's your choice."

"Oh you can't mean that," Darius said. "Sparky didn't hurt you. He simply tried to calm you down. He didn't bite or even rip your jacket. He's the gentlest dog I've ever known." He took a step forward, as if to shield Sparky.

"Oh yes I *do* mean it," she said. "That's my deal, take it or leave it. Your beast of a dog for my silence, and you and your friends are safe from being exposed... for now." Then she turned and started pedaling again. "Now I have work to do. I have to collect the rent over at the Marshal Farm, but I'll be around to your place to take that dog later this afternoon. You can count on it."

As she disappeared on the dusty, uneven road, Darius looked down at Sparky and smiled. He was the only real friend Darius had ever known and he'd helped get him through some of the darkest hours of his life. He couldn't imagine what he would do without Sparky and he couldn't let Agnes take him away like this. But more than that, even if Agnes didn't say anything about what she'd seen Darius and Jasper doing that afternoon, she now had information on Darius she could hold over his head for the rest of his life. There was no telling what she might do in the future. He would never be free of her now, and he would never close his eyes again without worrying that she might expose him.

Chapter Two

When Agnes was gone, Sparky looked up at Darius and licked his hand, as if he understood everything that had happened and he was trying to console him. Darius glanced down at the dog and smiled, and then he went down on one knee and put his arms around him. He hugged him tightly and said, "We have to figure this out, Sparky. We can't let that mean old woman take you away."

Sparky licked his face, and then Darius stood up to head back to his farm. The air was thick and hot and the sky was darker than he'd seen it in a long time. It was so humid his T-shirt was sticking to his chest and he wasn't even perspiring much. They were long overdue for rain and Darius knew the weather could become violent that time of year under these conditions. He tapped his thigh and said, "C'mon, Sparky, we'd better get back home and find Etienne and Nicola and warn them about Agnes McCain. They won't allow Agnes to take you away from me."

As if he were trying to tell Darius he agreed, the dog barked and they both set off toward the farm in a slow jog. Darius didn't want to waste a moment in his quest to save Sparky, and he wasn't even sure what he was going to tell his aunt and uncle when he did get home. He'd been lying to everyone... including himself... all his life about who he was and what he wanted to be. He knew he'd never grow up and marry a woman and have a family like other men. He knew he was different from other men and it wasn't just about sex. Sex was only part of who he was. The feelings he'd been hiding his entire life went much deeper than just sex.

The only way out of this mess with Agnes McCain was to tell the truth, which he was planning to do that afternoon the moment he returned home. He would tell his aunt and uncle that he'd been the one who had seduced the other guys and they were totally innocent. He didn't want to be responsible for ruining the lives of Jasper, Eddie and Tommy, and most of all he didn't want to lose his beloved dog, Sparky. He wasn't sure how Etienne and Nicola would react to this news about him seducing other men, or even if they would understand. He was hoping they would support him and stand up to Agnes McCain, but he wasn't expecting anything. He'd grown up with so much shame and self-loathing he wouldn't have blamed Etienne and Nicola if they threw him out of their home and disowned him completely. And he knew there was a strong chance they might do just that.

A few minutes later, they reached a dirt road that would lead them to the barn where he knew Etienne and Nicola would be working to prepare for the approaching storm. The sky was growing darker and the air had become dead still, a sign of troubled times ahead. On a farm there were routines and patterns that had to be followed, especially when it came to the animals. They had to be sheltered and protected, and equipment had to be stored away properly. Darius' own mother and father had perished in a twister and his family had almost lost the entire farm that day.

He rounded a corner and found Etienne and Nicola fixing a fence where they kept the goats. "Etienne, Etienne," Darius called out, "Something's happened and I have to speak to you right away. It's terrible. It's the worst possible thing that could ever happen. It involves that mean old Agnes McCain, and something that happened this afternoon. We have to talk this minute."

Etienne handed a hammer to Nicola. S he didn't even look up at Darius. "It's okay, dear. We're very busy right now with this storm coming. We can talk later." She was a short woman with long gray hair pulled back into a chignon. Her knee length calico dress was bunched up around her waist, like all her other dresses do, especially now that she had grown a little thicker around the middle in the last few years.

She clearly didn't realize how serious this was. "But Etienne," Darius said, "this is bad. This is very, very bad. Agnes McCain wants to take Sparky away from me and put him down."

Nicola finished hammering a nail into the fence and said, "She's the nastiest old woman I've ever set eyes on. I wouldn't worry about her." Nicola was portly, and he'd lost most of his hair by now. He had a tendency to pull his pants up above his waistline and belt them just below his chest. There was nothing confrontational about Nicola and he usually deferred to Etienne when it came to family matters of this nature.

"But you don't understand," Darius said. "I really have to talk to you. She means business this time and she wants to take Sparky away and have him put down. There's something you need to know about me. We have to talk."

Etienne still hadn't looked up at him. She was checking other parts of the fence to make sure they were secure enough for the goats. "We'll talk about this later, Darius. We have too much work to do right now. Stop being so dramatic, again. You know how you get sometimes, dear. Always dramatic. Just calm down. We just don't have time for histrionics at the moment. We'll sit down and talk later over a nice cup of tea."

They were always telling Darius he tended to be too dramatic, but this time it was different. He threw his arms in the air and turned in the opposite direction. He could see it was pointless to continue speaking. They were working hard and he knew he'd never get them to listen. He also knew it was pointless to ask if he could do anything to help prepare for the storm. His aunt and uncle had coddled him and spoiled him to the point where he'd never done a day of manual labor in his life. They'd been strict in the sense that they expected him to perform in school and plan for his future. They wanted him to go to college and make something of his life. This was part of the reason why they'd never expected him to do manual labor on the farm. He did have chores, and he worked hard doing his share. He was expected to work inside the farm house doing things like washing and ironing sheets and cleaning floors. He knew how to cook, how to clean an old stove, and how to bleach the tile grout. But for some reason he'd never been able to totally understand, they would not allow him to do any farm work whatsoever. They told him it was for his own good and he never complained. They'd been so good to him. They'd made it clear that they didn't want Darius to live the same lives they'd led.

He loved them so much he couldn't argue with them anymore. He knew he would have to tell them everything eventually and he didn't want to make their lives more difficult than they already were. So he headed toward the barn to see if he could help out over there, where Jasper, Eddie and Tommy would be. They would let Darius help. Etienne and Nicola thought nothing of paying part time help to come work on the farm, but they still wouldn't allow Darius to do a single thing when it came to manual labor.

This is why he had to talk to them, and to explain the entire situation so that Agnes McCain wouldn't destroy them all first. He headed toward the barn where the other guys were working and decided he would tell his aunt and uncle everything as soon as they stopped working outside.

He found Jasper heading in his direction. He was pulling a wagon that had to be stored safely in the barn. The instant Jasper saw Darius he stopped walking and began to stutter. He was still so worked up about Agnes catching them together that he stuttered so much it was difficult to understand him. "Darius this is bad. I can't let this get out. If my family and my girlfriend find out, I'm done. What we were doing was wrong. I'm not like you."

"I'll take care of everything," Darius said. "You have nothing to worry about, Jasper. Stop thinking about it. I'm going to take the blame for everything. I'll tell them I seduced you and it was all my fault. She has no proof about Tommy and Eddie so they have nothing to worry about either. You're the only one and I'll make sure I take all the blame. I don't mind."

"Are you sure? You don't mind?" Jasper asked, as if he didn't know how to react.

Darius nodded. "I'm sure. I don't mind taking the blame. Right after I tell Etienne and Nicola I've decided I'm leaving Uranus for good. I'm taking Sparky with me. I don't have any other choice. It's the best thing to do for everyone. You'll be okay. I promise."

"You're a great guy," Jasper said. He was still stuttering, but now Darius could at least understand him.

"So are you, Jasper, and don't you ever forget that," Darius said. He thought it was important to say this aloud. "You're a great guy, too, and we didn't do anything wrong. And no matter what happened, no matter what horrible people like Agnes McCain say, I want you to remember that. Do you understand? We did nothing wrong."

Jasper glanced down and shook his head. "I understand, but the rest of the world doesn't understand."

Darius looked at him and frowned.

Then Jasper turned and pulled the wagon toward the barn, with his head down and his jaw clenched, and Darius went down to see what Eddie and Tommy were doing near the old chicken coop.

He found them boarding up the side of the chicken coop to protect the chickens from the approaching storm. The sky was getting darker and they were working fast, but joking around at the same time. They knew nothing about what had happened with Agnes and Darius wasn't going to tell them. They were in the same situation as Jasper, with girlfriends and families. Darius saw no need to worry them. If Agnes did mention their names to anyone, and if she did make any accusations, Darius would call her a liar to her face. She'd never seen Darius do anything with either Eddie or Tommy, and she couldn't prove a thing. Of course Darius had been with both of them and they'd always been discreet. This was their private business and no one else had to know about it, and if he had to lie for survival he would do that.

When they glanced up and saw Darius approaching, Eddie smiled and said, "There he is. We've been wondering where you've been. Looks like bad weather is coming."

Eddie was the friendly one, and he was incredibly smart. He was tall and lanky, with reddish blond hair and broad shoulders and he'd always treated Darius with absolute respect. Darius trusted them both and he didn't think it would hurt if he told part of the story. "It's been awful today. Agnes McCain and I got into a scuffle and Sparky grabbed her arm. He didn't hurt her. He just wanted to stop her from screaming at me. And you know how she feels about dogs. She hates them. So now she's coming over here this afternoon to take Sparky away and have him put down."

Eddie shook his head. "That mean old bag. Someone should take her away and put her down."

Tommy glanced up from what he was hammering and asked, "What are you going to do, Darius?"

Darius shook his head. "I don't know, guys. I'm probably just going to run away. I'll leave town and take Sparky with me."

"Well that makes no sense," Eddie said. He looked up at the dark sky as if he were trying to figure out the most logical solution for Darius.

Although Darius knew it didn't make sense on the surface, he knew there was more to the story and he couldn't mention it to them. "I don't see any other way out. She's not taking Sparky."

Tommy looked up and said, "I can take care of Agnes. No one will ever find out." Tommy was the mean one. He had those dark good looks, with dark eyes and a heavy dark beard. His body was stocky and firm and hairy. No one would ever have suspected he'd been fooling around with Darius, too.

Darius smiled and said, "Thanks, Tommy, but you know how I feel about that. I don't want to harm her, as evil as she is. I could never live with myself."

"You're too nice," Tommy said. He made a fist and laughed. "Just say the word and I'll take care of things. You'll never have to worry about her again."

Darius took a step back and said, "I'll figure this out on my own, guys. I'm going to head to the house to see if there's anything to do there. I'll catch you later."

As Darius took another step back, he tripped over a rock and fell backward on to a huge pile of hay. Eddie and Tommy both stopped what they were doing and ran over to see if he was okay. Tommy reached down for his arm and said, "Let me help you up." Without even waiting for Darius to reply, he then reached down with both hands, lifted him up effortlessly, and held him in his arms.

While Eddie brushed off Darius' back, Darius pressed his palms to Tommy's strong chest and said, "I feel so stupid now. I can't even stand on my own two feet."

Before Tommy could reply, Etienne came over with a few leftover biscuits from lunch and said, "What's going on here?"

Of course they weren't doing anything sexual, but the way Tommy was holding Darius could have been misunderstood. So Darius pushed Tommy away fast. Tommy released him so quickly he almost fell backward.

Eddie spoke first. "Darius missed his step and fell backward. We were just helping him get up, is all."

Etienne stopped and looked them all up and down, as if she didn't believe them, and said, "Well, thank you for that, Tommy, but Darius is a big boy and I'm sure he can stand up on his own. You two get back to work. I brought you over some leftover biscuits. This storm is getting closer and there's still a lot of work to do."

When Etienne wasn't looking, Tommy reached around and patted Darius' buttocks and said, "We'll get right back to work, Etienne. We'll get this all done as fast as possible." Then he winked at Darius and reached for a biscuit.

Darius smiled and looked down at his shoes. He could tell Etienne wasn't mad at anyone. She just wanted to make sure everyone was working to get the place ready for the storm. Even though there was nothing outwardly unusual about Darius, everyone knew he wasn't the sturdiest man on the farm. It's not that he was weak, and he always came across as all man, it's just that there was something more delicate about him than other men his age.

Jasper, Eddie, and Tommy treated Darius differently than they treated each other. They were all more aggressive than he was and when they had sex with Darius they were always the ones on top of him. Of course Darius never questioned this because it all just seemed perfectly natural to all of them. Darius didn't consider himself weaker than the other guys either. In many ways Darius was tougher than they were and he knew that. He'd always been secure with them climbing on top of him and he'd never felt awkward about the fact that he'd always been the one to service their needs. The only downside was that they tended to treat him as if he were fragile, without even considering the fact that he was stronger than he appeared. He didn't resent them for this and he never complained. He knew they meant well and that they thought they were protecting him.

They returned to the chicken coop and Etienne turned to head back toward the house. Darius and Sparky ran after her and Darius said, "Agnes McCain is going to come here and she's going to take Sparky. And I won't let her. You have to listen to me, Etienne."

"Oh Darius, please stop being so dramatic," Etienne said. "We have so much to do and so little time left. This storm is coming fast. We can talk about this later."

He stopped, and Etienne continued toward the house. He knew there was nothing he could say or do at that point to make her listen, and he would just have to wait and see if Agnes showed up to take Sparky away.

Chapter Three

"Hey, Darius, get over here and help me in the barn. I need you real bad. Oh, real bad."

Darius turned and saw Eddie standing in the doorway of the broken down old barn. He had a cigarette in one hand and his other hand was on his hip. "I'll be right over," Darius said. He looked down and told Sparky to go back to the house and wait for him there.

Darius turned toward the barn and frowned. Even though Etienne and Nicola worked hard to maintain the farm, their funds were limited so the entire place always appeared unkempt and shabby no matter how much work they did. Everything was neatly and cleanly organized but the buildings were left in shambles. The white two-story farmhouse hadn't been painted in years and the paint that was there was chipped and pee ling. The outbuildings had never been painted and some were so old they were leaning sideways as if ready to come down. If only they had more money, the farm could do more than survive. One day, Darius swore, he would do something with his life and help restore the old farm to what it had once been.

When he reached the barn doorway, Eddie dropped the cigarette and stomped it out with his big cowboy boot. He sent Darius one of his seductive glances and said, "There you are."

"What can I do for you?" Darius asked. He had a feeling, but he didn't like to assume anything with guys like Eddie.

Eddie turned and Darius followed him inside. The moment they were out of sight, Eddie grabbed him by the waist and pulled him up against his warm sweaty body. "This is what you can do for me." Then he kissed Darius so hard on the mouth they both fell backward into a stall that was filled with hay.

A second or two later, Darius stopped kissing him and said, "We have to stop. We could get caught. Tommy is right outside and my aunt and uncle are right up front. Anyone could catch us. I'm in enough trouble as it is with Agnes McCain."

Eddie reached around and put his hand down Darius' pants. "That's what makes it more fun. Take off your pants, Darius. You know you want to."

Even though Darius hadn't planned on this, he knew Eddie well enough to know that it wouldn't take long. Tall, lanky red-headed Eddie always knew what he wanted and he never disappointed Darius in the process of getting it. He was a fast lover, with a long, thick penis. His girlfriend in town had made it clear she would remain a virgin until she got married so Eddie couldn't turn to her with his strong needs. Eddie seemed fine with that and he turned to Darius to satisfy him instead. Although Darius often wondered about this to himself, he never questioned Eddie about it because he suspected it was the same old story, as usual. Men like Darius and Eddie weren't allowed to discuss their feelings aloud. They were expected to behave a certain way in public, but what they did in private was always discreet and unmentioned. In other words, Darius suspected that Eddie was just as attracted to other men as he was, but he would never admit that to himself or to anyone else aloud. He would simply go through life having sex with men on the sly and pretend in public to be just like every other man out here in the world.

The only thing different about Darius when compared to Eddie, Jasper and Tommy was that Darius wanted more out of life, and he was more comfortable with who he was. He didn't want to pretend to be like other men and sneak around for the rest of his life. He didn't want to pretend to be with a woman. Darius wanted to fall in love with one man, spend his life with one man, and live with that one man as if they were a married couple. Even though he wasn't sure that was possible, he never fooled himself into believing that he could pretend to be anything else.

On that afternoon, with Eddie on top of him and Eddie's hand down his pants, Darius knew he had needs of his own. He'd always been attracted to Eddie's reddish brown hair and his lean solid body. He'd always liked the way Eddie treated him so kindly and with so much respect. He couldn't have said no to him that afternoon if his life had depended on it. Of course that was a big part of Darius' problems: he never could say no to any of the guys.

While Eddie pulled down his zipper and Darius pulled down his pants, Darius said, "We have to do this quickly, Eddie. We can't get caught."

Eddie nodded. "It won't take long. I promise."

After Darius removed his pants and spread his legs,

Eddie climbed on top of him and entered him slowly. They'd already been together enough times to avoid any awkward moments. Eddie knew how to lubricate Darius with his saliva and Darius knew how to take Eddie by relaxing the most important parts of his body for this particular act. Eddie entered him slowly and Darius reached up with both hands to hold the back of Eddie's neck. As Eddie slid in deeper, Darius closed his eyes and said, "Oh that feels so good, Eddie."

Eddie grunted and said, "You're the best, Darius."

Then Eddie began moving his hips and Darius spread his legs wider. Darius not only welcomed him to continue, he encouraged him each time he stroked the back of his neck gently. The entire encounter lasted less than 10 minutes and by the time they were both finished Eddie rested on top of Darius and said, "Thanks, Darius, I needed that, pal."

Darius ran his hands up and down Eddie's back and said, "So did I, Eddie, so did I." In fact, he felt so good at that moment he would have started singing a song about rainbows and happy little bluebirds if he'd had a halfway decent voice. He also didn't know any good songs about rainbows or happy little bluebirds.

A few minutes after that, they stood up and Darius put his pants on fast. As Eddie turned to leave, he slapped Darius on the butt playfully and said, "I'll see you later. I've got to get back to work."

Darius heard Sparky barking and he said, "I'd better go see why he's barking. I'll see you later, too."

On his way back to the old farm house, Darius thought about how amazing it was that these encounters always happened so fast. It hadn't always been that way. In the beginning, back when Darius had first started fooling about with the farm hands on the sly, he'd been apprehensive about doing certain things with men. He'd learned everything he knew about being with a man by proverbial trial and error, and that hadn't always been easy. Even though his dream was to meet a man, fall in love, and live happily ever after, he wasn't so sure that would ever happen for him. So he took pleasure in knowing that he could at least be with a man on occasion, without having to make a big deal of it. He couldn't lie to himself either. He enjoyed being with Eddie, Tommy and Jasper as much as they claimed they enjoyed him. The best part about all of this is that each man was unique. Tommy was the rough and serious one. He took Darius from behind and slammed him into walls. Eddie was kinder and gentler, and he gently placed Darius on his back and treated him as if he were special. And then there was Jasper. He was awkward, and unsure of himself. He fucked the way he spoke: awkward with a stammer. And each time he was with Darius something different happened. There was nothing wrong with that, and Jasper was always so thankful afterward that it warmed Darius' heart.

As he grew closer to the house, Sparky's barking grew more intense. This wasn't his normal b ark either. This odd bark sounded as though he was in distress and he was calling for help. Then Darius saw Etienne running toward the house and he called out her name. "Etienne, Etienne, what's wrong?" When she didn't stop and reply, he started jogging.

By the time he reached the back door, he heard voices from the living room and Sparky was still barking. He raced inside, through the kitchen and into the dining room, and he found Etienne and Nicola in the parlor with Agnes McCain. There was a rope around Sparky's neck which made Darius sick to his stomach. Sparky had never been tethered with a rope a day in his life. He had a leash and a collar, but never a rope. Etienne and Agnes were tugging at it. While Nicola just stood there watching the women shout at each other, Darius walked up to them and tried to take the rope into his own hands.

As Darius reached for the rope, Agnes gave it one quick tug and pulled it out of Etienne's hands. She took a step back away from Darius and said, "I'm taking this beast with me now and I'm having him put down. That animal attacked me today and I have an order from the sheriff's office making it very much legal."

Agnes pulled a piece of paper out of her jacket pocket and handed it to Etienne. While Etienne looked it over, Agnes said, "You can read it with your own eyes, Etienne. It's right there in black and white."

Darius felt even sicker now. He knew Agnes not only owned more than half the county, but she also controlled the sheriff and politicians. He knew she could get them to do anything for her, whether it was legal or not.

Etienne glanced up from the paper she was reading and said, "How much did this cost you, Agnes? I know how crooked you are."

Agnes squared her back. "Are you insinuating that I bribed a public official to get that, Etienne? Because if you are, I'll go get the sheriff and bring him right back here with me and you can tell him that in person."

Etienne took a deep breath and sighed as though she were restraining herself from committing an act of violence. She glanced at Darius and shrugged her shoulders. As she handed the piece of paper back to Agnes, she looked her in the eye and said, "I've never liked you, Agnes McCain. You're an abusive bully, you're heartless, and you're just as ugly on the outside as you are on the inside. And those are your *best* qualities, you dried up old hag."

Nicola snickered and glanced in the other direction. Apparently, he wasn't going to get involved with two women fighting, but he didn't seem upset with Etienne.

Agnes turned and sent a vicious glance in Nicola's direction. "And what are you laughing at, you *fairy*. Sometimes I think all those feminine permanent waves you get every three months have gone to your brain."

"*That* will be enough, Agnes McCain," said Etienne. Her fists were clenched and her back squared, as though she was ready to jump on Agnes's back. "You say one more disparaging word against my husband and I swear on my Bible it will be your *last* word."

Everything stopped and there was a long moment of silence. Everyone knew Nicola tended to be slightly effeminate, and that he took a permanent wave at the local beauty parlor. But that had no reflection on the kind of good man he was or the kind of husband he was. He and Etienne had a good marriage. Darius had seen that for himself first hand. They were both truly devoted to each other as husband and wife, and if there was anything about his basic personality that went deeper with Nicola it was no one's business. So when Agnes McCain called him a fairy, Etienne lost all her reserve and forgot all her proper manners.

As Agnes opened her mouth to speak, Etienne cut her off. "You have the nerve to call people names, you dried up old witch of a woman. You have the gall to use that tone when referring to my husband that not only hurts him, but also many other men like him. You're nothing to me, Agnes McCain. You're nothing at all, other than a hollow shell of a human being and no one in this county can stomach you. And I'll tell you one more thing, Agnes McCain, you'll die alone someday. And when you do, I will go to your funeral wearing a bright white dress and I will dance on top of your grave. Now get the *hell* out of my house or I'll take you by the back of the neck and kick your flat skinny *ass* right out the door."

"Well, no one has *ever* spoken to me that way," Agnes said.

Etienne looked her in the eye and lowered her voice. "Oh, yes they have."

Nicola snickered again and sat down in his easy chair. He seemed to have learned how to accept himself years ago and women like Agnes McCain meant nothing to him.

"Well I'm finished," Agnes said, turning to leave. She yanked on the rope and said, "I'm taking this beast over to the pound right now where they will take care of him so no one is ever attacked again."

Darius reached for the rope and said, "No. I won't let you do that. You can't take him."

Etienne frowned. "I'm sorry, Darius. The dried up old bat has the legal right to do it. There's nothing we can do."

Darius' heart was racing by then. He knew he couldn't stop this from happening and he'd never felt so hopeless in his life. He glanced at Etienne, and then at Nicola, hoping they might still be able to do something. And when he saw there was nothing more they could do, he glowered at Agnes and said, "You're the fairy. You're a wicked evil fairy."

Agnes cast a glare in his direction. "What did you say? Would you like to repeat that?"

He knew she could have done worse that afternoon. She could have exposed him and told his aunt and uncle that she'd caught him having sex with Jasper at the Riggleby farm. She would have ruined everyone's life, including Jasper's. Darius wanted to come out with the truth right there and then to his aunt and uncle before Agnes had the chance, but his heart started pounding faster and he couldn't bring himself to say the words aloud. As much as he wanted to be truthful about who he was, the shame was still too strong for him to process, and the fear too intense. He knew that if he admitted the truth about himself he could never take it back. He would be that man… the pervert… who had sex with other men for the rest of his life. He would be all the vulgar words and references they said about men like him. Agnes had placed him in the worst possible position and there was nothing left for him to do but run out of the room, down the hall to his bedroom, and slam the door behind him.

Chapter Four

He fell across a small twin bed that had been pushed up against the wall and he heard more shouting in the parlor. He suspected Etienne was still arguing with Agnes and their voices grew shriller with each comment they made. The shouting didn't last long and the next sound he heard was the front door slam shut. A second after that, he heard Agnes start the engine of her pick-up truck. Darius glanced out the window above his bed and watched her pull away from the house with Sparky standing in the flatbed of the truck, watching the farm disappear in the distance and wagging his tail.

His heart crumbled in his chest and he buried his face in his pillow. He knew there was nothing he could do at that point and it would be the last time he would ever see Sparky. He thought about going back into the parlor to tell Etienne and Nicola the truth about himself, and maybe there was still time to save Sparky from being put down. Then he sighed aloud and closed his eyes. He couldn't do that to them, not even to save Sparky, and not under these conditions. Agnes had won and she'd gotten what she wanted and he knew he would have to learn to live with this for the rest of his life. His eyes felt heavy and he didn't care about the storm or anything else. He rested his head on the pillow, closed his eyes, and drifted off into a deep sleep without even trying too hard.

The next thing he heard was barking coming from the window above his head. At first, he thought he was dreaming and he didn't want to open his eyes. Then the barking grew louder and he opened his eyes and glanced up. He saw Sparky's head poking through the open window and he was trying to get into the bedroom. Darius stood up and threw his arms around Sparky's neck. "You escaped. I can't believe you're here. I never thought I'd see you again." He figured Agnes must have stopped at an intersection and Sparky jumped out of the flatbed and ran all the way home. It probably never even crossed Agnes's mind that Sparky would be smart enough to do something like this. People who don't like dogs always underestimate them.

Sparky barked and Darius' expression tightened. He looked at Sparky and said, "First I'm going to get that rope off you, and then we've got to get out of here. We're leaving Uranus and never coming back. It's time, Sparky. I'm not going to let Agnes McCain have you put down, and that means that she's going to expose me to them. And I can't tell them myself because it would ruin them. So the only thing left to do is leave. It's the best thing for everyone."

He didn't give himself time to think about anything. He reached under the bed, pulled out an old duffle bag, and started shoving his clothes and belongings into it. He grabbed whatever he could find first, without thinking about what he was packing. He knew Agnes would return looking for Sparky and he didn't want to be there when she did. He didn't even leave a note for Etienne and Nicola because there wasn't enough time. He would send them a letter of apology and let them know he was okay. The instant he pulled the zipper on his duffle bag shut he climbed out the window, removed the rope around Sparky's neck, and headed for the main road that would lead him out of town.

The sky continued to grow darker with each step he took. Darius knew he was walking directly toward the storm. It couldn't be avoided. He couldn't go in the other direction because he might have run into Agnes if he did. At least he wasn't alone. He had Sparky.

About a mile down the dusty old road that would lead him out of town, he heard someone whistling a tuneless song and he stopped and glanced to his right. He spotted an old wooden carnival wagon down a narrow side road hidden in between overgrown trees and weeds. It was one of those old-fashioned box-shaped enclosed wagons that could be hitched to the back of a pick-up truck, and then he saw an old blue pick-up truck parked between a few trees and overgrown weeds. It reminded him of the enclosed wagons he'd seen whenever the travelling circus passed through town, only this one was much shabbier and less colorful.

He turned and took a few steps toward the wagon so he could read the writing that had been stenciled across the side. In large faded white print the first line read, "The Marvelous Fantastical Doctor Salvation." Beneath that it read, "Let Dr. Salvation Help You Find Your Perfect Mate." Then, in smaller faded print, Darius saw a list of things that ranged from reading fortunes to selling love potions. His eyes grew wider when he saw that everyone was welcome to learn more about Dr. Salvation and these magical promises. He walked right up to see if there was more information about the love potions.

Of course Etienne and Nicola would have said this Dr. Salvation was nothing more than a snake oil salesman with a gimmick out to take the hard earned money of good-natured trusting fools. If someone pulling a wagon like this with the name Dr. Salvation had pulled up to the farm peddling this brand of silliness they would have run him off with their shotgun. But Darius was in no position to question anything at that point. He was running away from home, without any direction or money in his pocket, and he thought fate had led him to Dr. Salvation.

As he approached the side of the wagon where all the faded stenciled writing was located, the whistling stopped and a tall, attractive man with dark hair hopped out of the back. He must have been shaving because he had a white towel in one hand and an old fashioned razor in the other. Darius blinked and said, "I'm sorry. I didn't mean to intrude."

The tall man with dark hair smiled and said, "No problem. I'm at your service. Let me know what I can do for you." It didn't seem to bother him that he wasn't wearing anything but white underwear in the presence of a guest as he made no attempt whatsoever to put on his clothes.

Darius had never seen a more beautiful man in his entire life, and he felt an instant connection. His dark hair was thick and wavy, his shoulders broad and solid, and he had just the right amount of hair on his legs. Even though his skin was smooth and he had a silver loop in his right ear lobe, there was nothing delicate about him. His chest muscles protruded through his thin white cotton undershirt, and there was a huge bulge in the crotch of his sheer white cotton undershorts. Darius wasn't sure whether to gulp and run back to the road, or fall down on his knees and yank his dick out of his underwear.

"There has to be something I can do for you," the man said. "I don't see nice-looking young men like you come around all the time. Just tell me what you want and I'll do it. Your wish is my command."

He spoke with an eloquent voice and perfect diction, which lead Darius to believe he was highly educated. He didn't have a hint of that folksy country accent everyone else had in Uranus. It gave him a unique air of sophistication that made him even more attractive. Darius looked into his deep dark eyes and said, "Your sign says that you know the future, Dr. Salvation. I guess I'd like to know about my future."

He reached out to shake Darius' hand and said, "I'm Kit Lawler. That's what all my close friends call me. It's a pleasure to meet someone so handsome, refined, and smart."

Darius shook his hand and said, "Well I don't know about all *that*, but I'm Darius Krasner and this is my dog, Sparky. It's nice to meet you, too, Kit." He was so attracted to this tall dark man his heart was ready to bust from his chest. This was the tall dark man of his dreams, the man he never thought he would meet in person, and the man he could fall in love with. Darius had stood on the sidelines all his life watching things happen to everyone else around him, and now here he was living his own dream come true.

Up until that moment he didn't even know there were men like this in Uranus. Kit seemed different from men like Jasper, Eddie and Tommy. They were only interested in their physical needs, and then they would return to their families and girlfriends. It was different with Kit. There was an aura of self-confidence around Kit that suggested he knew who he was and he wasn't ashamed of it, especially not with Darius.

"Why don't we go over there and sit on that nice bench and I'll read your palm for you," Kit said. "I'm not sure what I'll find, and I may not be very good at it, but I have strong feelings about you. I feel as if we've already met before but I'm not sure where. I can't explain how I feel."

"I've never had my palm read before," Darius said. "But I am curious." He'd heard about palm readers and fortune tellers and he'd seen them at carnivals. He'd just never actually been to one. Etienne and Nicola were no nonsense kind of people. If they even thought he'd been to a palm reader they would have gone into a long lecture about fakes and shady people. And normally Darius would have listened to their advice because deep down he didn't really believe in palm readers or fortune tellers either. But a small part of him wanted to believe in something that day, and he'd been so frightened by Agnes McCain he needed something to believe.

He followed Kit over to a narrow unpainted wooden bench that looked as old and weather beaten as the faded wooden wagon. There was an exotic looking handmade carpet in reds, gold, greens, blues, and black hanging on a tree branch with a sign that read: *Magic Carpet Rides*. He'd only read about magic carpets in books and he'd never seen one before. He wanted to ask more about it, but he didn't want to sound obtuse. So

Darius sat down first and then Kit sat down next to him so closely their knees touched. Darius couldn't stop staring at Kit's strong hairy legs or the bulge in his white undershorts. While he was sitting, at this angle, Darius could actually see the outline of his penis.

"Give me your hand," Kit said. He looked directly into Darius' eyes and smiled.

Darius extended his arm and turned his hand palm side up. "Is this okay?"

Kit took Darius' hand in his hands and he smiled again. "It's perfect. You're perfect." Then he ran one hand up and down Darius' arm slowly and said, "You have very soft, delicate skin. You're so beautiful."

Darius gulped. He wasn't sure how to respond. "Ah well, thanks."

Kit stared down at Darius' palm without saying a word. He ran his index finger all around Darius' palm without uttering a single word. After about a minute or two, he looked up and said, "I see that you're distressed. You're not happy about something right now, and that's why you're leaving your home and all the people who care about you."

Of course at the time it didn't occur to Darius that Kit had seen his duffle bag, so he opened his eyes wider and said, "Yes. That's exactly what's happening. I have to leave town right away and I can't tell anyone why I'm leaving."

"There's some trouble in your home, with your family," Kit said.

Darius nodded. "Why yes. That's exactly what's happening. It's uncanny that you can see all this."

Kit sent him a smile and shrugged. "It's a good thing you ran into me," he said. "I may be able to help.

35

But I have to get to know more about you. Are you willing to go inside the wagon for a more intense reading?"

Darius was so attracted to him by then he would have followed him up a tree. He couldn't think of anything more he'd rather do. He nodded and said, "I'll go inside with you. I'd like to learn more about you, too, Kit." This time he reached down and he ran his fingers across Kit's hairy leg to show just how interested he was.

"We should go inside, then," Kit said. He didn't flinch at all when Darius touched his leg. "We can continue to get to know each other better in there."

By the time they stood up from the bench, Darius glanced down at Kit's crotch and noticed he had a full erection now, and he made no attempt to hide it. He pointed and said, "What on Earth is *that*?" He didn't care about sounding obtuse now.

Kit knew he was joking, so he played along. "That's what you've done to me. It's your entire fault."

Darius reached for his hand and said, "Then we'd better get inside fast. There's not a moment to waste."

They started kissing the moment they reached the entrance of the old wooden wagon. Darius threw his arms around Kit's large broad shoulders and Kit grabbed him by the waist. The kissing was different for Darius because the farm hands he'd slept with had never really liked to kiss much. They'd always been more interested in what Darius could do to service them, without reciprocation. Kit was different in that respect. He seemed to want to please Darius as much as Darius wanted to please him.

They continued to kiss outside the wagon. Kit

grabbed Darius' waist and lifted him up so he could climb into the wagon. It was dark inside because there were no windows, but it smelled like musk and it was so clean he didn't see a speck of dust anywhere. There was an old-fashioned table with two hand-carved old chairs on one end, and a neatly made bed on the other end that had been covered with a red velvet spread. The red velvet spread looked so inviting that Darius turned and started to remove his clothes without even thinking about Kit. He couldn't wait to climb up on the red velvet spread, naked. For the first time in his life he would be with a man... a real man... without having to hide in hay in a dirty old barn with the stench of cow manure.

He pulled off his shirt fast and tossed it on the floor. As he was about to unfasten his pants, Kit said, "What are you doing?"

Darius turned and he saw Kit sitting on one of the hand carved chairs at the table. He was still in his underwear and he hadn't removed anything yet. He shrugged and said, "I was taking off my clothes for you. That's what the farm hands like me to do. I don't mind. I want to do it. I want you to climb on top of me and I want you to do whatever you want to do. I like you."

Kit laughed and said, "Well, Darius, I like you, too. In fact, I like you so much I'd like to get to know you a little better before I just climb on top of you and do whatever I want. I don't operate that way, especially when I really like someone special. Come over here and sit down on a chair so I can get to know you better and talk about your feelings. I'm in no rush."

"Are you sure? You actually want to talk about my feelings?"

"Of course I'm sure."

37

Darius shrugged and walked over to the table so he could sit down across from Kit. This was the first time a man had ever wanted to talk to him about his feelings. The farm hands treated him well, they were careful not to disrespect him, but none of them ever wanted to actually talk to him first. He wasn't sure how he felt about this, but he was curious about the crystal ball on the table.

When he was seated, he looked up and asked, "Are you really a doctor, a real doctor? Or are you just a traveling salesman with an interesting gimmick?"

Kit looked into his eyes and smiled. "I am a real doctor. I'd heard they needed a doctor in this county and that's why I came all this way. I've been traveling for a long time. This wagon and everything else belonged to my grandmother. She was actually Doctor Salvation, and she raised me and put me through school reading palms and telling fortunes. She taught me everything I need to know and that's how I've been making money while working my way through school. My real goal is to settle down in a nice little place like Uranus and be a country doctor. I wouldn't lie to you about that. I went to medical school in Chicago and I really am a doctor."

"Oh I believe you, Kit," Darius said. "I would believe anything you tell me."

"Well that's a mistake," Kit said. "What if I'm not telling the truth? I could be just another salesman taking advantage of you. You shouldn't be so trusting. That makes me worry."

Darius reached for his hand and he squeezed it gently. "Well I'm not all that trusting. I know there are plenty of horrible men and women out there, but I do

38

trust *you*. I don't think you'd lie to me. I can see it in your eyes, and I can feel it."

After that, they remained at the table for a few minutes while Kit glanced into the crystal ball and read Darius' future. Darius knew Kit was only stating broad generalities about his life, but it was amusing and they actually did get to know each other a little better. Darius told him about his life on the farm and about how he'd lost his parents. He mentioned Etienne and Nicola and how they'd raised him as if he'd been their own child. Kit went into a brief explanation about how he'd been raised by his maternal grandmother who'd spent a good deal of her life in caravans traveling with carny people. She wasn't a real doctor and she never pretended to be one. She'd scrimped and saved every penny so he could go to school and study to become a real doctor and she didn't live long enough to see him graduate. Although he sounded strong and upbeat and positive, there was also something sad about him that pierced Darius' heart.

He felt so connected to Kit he finally reached over and grabbed his hand. "Let's go over to the bed now. It's hard for me to tell you how I feel, but I can show you how I feel."

They both stood without saying a word and by the time they reached the bed Darius was naked. He slowly climbed up on the red velvet bed cover and turned around so he could face Kit. He was still standing beside the bed. Darius reached for the waistband of his white undershorts. He slipped them down Kit's hairy legs, slowly, so that Kit could step out of them, and so he could wrap his hand around Kit's erection.

Kit removed his underwear shirt and glanced down. He watched Darius open his mouth and set his lips to the head of his penis and start sucking slowly. When Darius glanced up at him, with most of Kit's penis in his mouth, their eyes locked and Kit caressed the top of his head. Then he nodded and said, "You're so beautiful. I have to be very careful with you."

Darius didn't respond. They didn't need words at that point. He started sucking his dick with more intensity and he eventually brought him so close to climax Kit had to grab Darius' head and hold it still. As if he could read his mind, Darius stopped sucking and he rested back on the bed slowly. When he was flat on his back, he lifted his legs and he spread them so that Kit could climb up on the bed and enter him. He still felt that strong connection that he'd never experienced before with his buddies on the farm. This was more emotional and Darius didn't totally understand it. He simply knew that he wanted to continue making love to this unusual stranger, and he didn't want it to end.

Kit climbed on top of him and reached for baby oil on a shelf next to the bed. He rubbed the baby oil all over his erection and in between Darius' legs, and then he slipped his erection inside Darius' body so effortlessly Darius didn't even flinch. None of his farm hand fuck buddies had ever used a lubricant to fuck him and he'd simply learned how to accommodate them with saliva. The baby oil was new and different and it felt so smooth and slippery between his legs he lifted his arms, threw them around Kit's neck, and they started kissing so passionately Darius lost track of everything around him.

While Kit moved his pelvis evenly and gently, he slid in and out of Darius' body while kissing the entire time. Once again, this was nothing like being with the farm hands. Sex with men had always been good for Darius, but this was so much better with Kit. Darius held Kit's shoulders and Kit braced his palms beside Darius' shoulders. Kit moved faster with each thrust. At one point Darius reached down between his legs and grabbed his own erection while Kit continued to fuck him. A few minutes after that Kit grunted and slammed into him one last time. While Darius came on his own stomach, Kit remained still and he came inside Darius. They opened their eyes and exchanged a glance, and then Kit fell on top of him and he didn't get up until his penis slid out of Darius' body on its own.

While Darius remained breathless beneath Kit, pinned to the red velvet bed cover with his legs still spread apart, he caressed the back of Kit's neck gently and whispered something into his ear that he'd never said to any other man he'd known. "That was the most wonderful thing I have ever experienced. Please stay this way for a few more minutes. I want to memorize this moment so that I'll remember it until the day I die."

Chapter Five

When Kit finally did climb off Darius' body, a gust of strong wind rocked the old wooden wagon and it startled Sparky so much he jumped up and barked. "What on Earth was that?" Darius asked. He was still naked, flat on his back. He wanted to watch Kit walk around naked for a minute to two.

Kit shrugged and scratched his junk. "I guess it's the storm we've been waiting for."

Another strong gust of wind shook the wagon. Darius jumped up and climbed off the bed to find his pants. He felt this sudden need to run home but he wasn't sure why. It wasn't out of guilt because of what he'd just done with Kit. This was something stronger. He had this feeling that Etienne and Nicola were in trouble and he had to get back to the farm as quickly as possible.

His pants were nowhere in sight. He hated when this happened. He'd lost track of how many times he'd lost his pants this way. Kit didn't make it much better either. As Darius leaned over to look under the table to see if his pants were there, Kit reached down and grabbed his bottom in a playful way and said, "You should just stay here until the storm passes. It's too dangerous for you out there. I don't want you to go. If you leave and something happens I'll never forgive myself. Stay here and we can climb back into bed and weather this together."

He spotted his pants rolled up on a ball over where Sparky was sitting. As he crossed the wagon to get them, he said, "I have to go back. I know that sounds ridiculous, but I'm worried something is wrong."

He grabbed his pants, put them on, and then finished putting on the rest of his clothes. When he was dressed, he realized that in his rush to get dressed he'd forgotten to put on his underpants and socks. But it was too late for that now. He felt such a strong urge to leave he kissed Kit goodbye and said, "I have to go now. I hope I see you again. I really like you. Be careful. C'mon, Sparky. We have to run."

As if he could understand every word Darius said, Sparky jumped up and walked to the end of the wagon.

Kit grabbed Darius and held him for a moment. "Be safe. This looks bad."

"I will. I promise."

Kit kissed him one last time and asked, "I'm going to look for you when this is over."

"I hope so," Darius said. "I really like you and I want to see you again. I live at the farm a mile or so down the road. It's not that difficult to find anyone in Uranus."

Then Darius turned and jumped out of the wagon with Sparky not far behind. He ran to the main road, turned left, and ran all the way back to the farm. It wasn't easy because he was running against the wind and it was so strong it knocked him off balance a few times. He had to grab a few fence posts to continue, and the dust from the old dirt road kept getting in his eyes.

By the time he reached the road that would lead him back to the farm the sky had grown so dark it looked more like twilight than afternoon and he couldn't shake the bad feeling in the pit of his stomach.

As he grew closer to the house the wind grew even stronger. In the distance he heard a deep howling sound. An old wooden chair that had been on the front porch flew in his direction and missed him by inches. The old table where Etienne set her wash basket flew over his head. He watched it smash into the side of the barn. Shutters began to swing back and forth, anything that wasn't nailed or fastened to the ground started to blow in all directions, and the roof blew off the chicken coop and all the chickens jumped out and ran off in different directions. This wasn't just any old storm. This was worse. When he reached the back of the farmhouse and glanced up at the back pasture, he saw a huge dark funnel cloud heading directly for the farm.

"Etienne, Nicola." He shouted with such force his throat hurt. "Etienne, Nicola. Where are you?"

He thought they might be in the storm cellar so he ran to where the cellar doors were located and found them locked tightly. He tried to pull them open but it was no use. The wind was so strong and so loud by that point he started to shout again, hoping Etienne, Nicola, and the farm hands were safe and they could hear him. He kicked the cellar doors and said, "Etienne, Nicola, let me in. Please let me in. Etienne, Nicola."

No one responded. He turned and glanced toward the back pasture again. He pressed his palm to his mouth and gasped. He could see the dark funnel cloud was getting closer, heading directly toward his farm. He didn't want to run to the barn because that was the oldest building on the farm and that would be the first to come down. He couldn't just stand outside and hope for the best. He had one choice: he had to go into the house and find a safe place to hide. So he tapped his leg and said, "C'mon, Sparky. We have to hurry. There's no time."

They ran toward the house and climbed the back stairs two at a time. The screen door was already swinging back and forth in the wind. He had to be careful it didn't hit him in the face. He called out once again, "Etienne, Nicola, are you here?" No one replied. H e figured they'd already found shelter in the storm cellar and they couldn't hear him. He'd probably missed them by seconds.

He ran to the small bedroom on the first floor where he slept and Sparky followed. As he turned to close the bedroom door a huge gust of wind blew the window frame over his bed into his room so fast he didn't have time to dodge it. The old wooden window frame hit the side of his head and stunned him so suddenly he fell backward and landed on his back. The bed braced his fall, but he was covered with wood and glass and he lost track of everything else around him. He couldn't hear the wind blowing anymore, and the shutters that had been banging against the clapboards went silent. Then everything went dark and he felt a sense of peace and calm envelope him. And as he closed his eyes, not even thinking about the dark funnel cloud anymore, the last thing he felt was Sparky's head brushing up against his palm.

When he finally opened his eyes again and sat up, he felt a little dizzy and the house was rocking. It was a strange feeling, as if the house was moving in circles, but in slow motion. Sparky barked. Darius glanced out the window above his bed and pressed his palms to his chest. He saw chairs fly by, someone's sofa seemed to be drifting in mid-air, and the most beautiful naked man flew by and waved at him. He'd never seen this naked man before, but he felt as if he knew him. He had blond hair, a well-defined muscular body, and a thick chunky penis.

Darius wasn't sure what was happening so he rose from the bed and walked over to the window and glanced down. "We must be in the funnel cloud, Sparky. Right in the center of it."

He took a step back when he saw Agnes McCain drift by in her old pick-up truck. She had both hands gripped to the steering wheel and she was sitting up close to it, slightly hunched over. She looked into his bedroom window and sent him a quick sideways glance, and then she continued driving until she was out of sight. That's when the house started to rock and spin faster. The bed and the dresser moved away from the walls and he fell on the bed so he wouldn't fly out the window. The house felt as though it was falling and spinning totally out of control. He didn't know where he was headed or where he would wind up. The only thing he could do at that point was hold on to Sparky and cover his face with a pillow.

When the house finally landed with a thud, everything stopped moving. Darius stood up from the bed and looked around. Everything seemed to be okay now. The house hadn't fallen apart and Sparky was sitting on the bed staring at him. So he patted the top of Sparky's head and said, "Let's go out and take a look."

He opened the bedroom door slowly and crept down the hallway as if this was the first time he'd ever been inside this house. There were no signs of Etienne or Nicola and he figured they were still down in the storm cellar. He crossed through the dining room and then the living room slowly, as if each step he took could be his last. When he finally reached the front door he stood there staring at it for a moment because he was terrified to open it and see what was outside.

He squared his back and took a deep breath. As he opened the door, Darius exhaled and his eyes grew wide. The old farmhouse seemed to have landed somewhere odd, in a place he'd never been before. He'd never seen such a bright blue sky, so many exotic colorful flowers, and so many magnificent shades of green in his entire life. The shrubs were all perfectly pruned and the walkways all neatly swept. It was so exaggerated it didn't look real. It reminded him of a painting he'd once seen in a picture book about a far off land in a magical world of wonder.

As strange as all this was, he felt safe. He took a few steps forward and exited the house. To his right there was a shrub that seemed to have pink cotton candy growing on it, and to his left stood a tree with small droplets of milk chocolate hanging from its branches. They reminded him of acorns made out of chocolate and he wasn't sure if they were safe to eat. But the most amazing thing of all was the silver glittery path that was directly in front of him. The path had been gilded in silver with small specks of silver glitter, the kind of glitter he'd only seen on greeting cards during the holiday season. As he glanced up and looked forward, the silver path led to a pale blue bridge where there was a fountain that looked as if it was overflowing with sweet cherry soda.

Sparky barked and Darius looked at him and said, "I don't know where we are, but this place sure is different. I've never seen anything more beautiful. The street lamps are made out of lollipops, the grass is so green it looks fake, and the water in that pond beneath the blue bridge reminds me of pink lemonade. Where are we, Sparky? What is this place?"

Sparky barked again. Darius walked toward the magical blue bridge. On the other side of the bridge, he saw a cluster of buildings that reminded him of tiny doghouses. The roofs were made out of that old-fashioned thatch he'd seen in English picture books, and the walls had been painted in several different pastel shades. He saw pink, green, blue and yellow. There were several different shades of red, and even some purple. If something was white, it was pure white. And there were no signs of gray anywhere to be seen.

He thought he heard voices coming from a row of thick shrubs in the background, but when he turned all the way around he saw nothing and there was total silence. He faced the bridge and the cluster of tiny doghouses again and looked up at the clear blue sky. His jaw dropped. He couldn't move. There was something in the sky floating toward him. He blinked a few times because he couldn't believe what he was seeing. There was a giant, sparkling crystal chandelier descending from a puffy white cloud. It shimmered and glowed just like the chandeliers he'd seen in a fancy restaurant once. And as it came toward him, he glanced down at Sparky and said, "Oh Sparky, I don't know what this is, but I have a feeling we are not in *Uranus* anymore."

Chapter Six

When the sparkling chandelier reached the silver path, Darius saw a puff of silver glitter and a second later the most beautiful woman he'd ever seen from a distance materialized before his eyes. Her hair was long and blond and highlighted with silver sparkles. She wore a silver gown studded with crystals that had a long slit up the right side exposing her long shapely leg. Her silver stilettos matched her gown, and her earrings mimicked the large chandelier that had brought her down from the sky. She even had a large elaborate ring on every finger, long white manicured fingernails, and so much make up on her face it resembled marzipan.

While Darius stood there without saying a word, the woman took a step toward him, smiled in his direction, and asked, "Are you a good fairy or a bad fairy, doll?" She spoke with a deep, husky voice.

Darius gulped and said, "I don't know what that means." Even though she was dressed and made up like a woman she sounded like a man, with that deep throaty voice and those strong angular features. At a closer glance he had a feeling she was a man dressed as a woman and he didn't know how to react. He'd read once there were men who dressed as women and they were professional entertainers. Of course in his small world in Uranus that wasn't common knowledge. He'd only read about it by accident while browsing through a bookstore on a class trip to the state capital. But most important, he knew deep down inside they shared something in common. He was still too young to put this into words, but all his instincts told him they were connected.

"Well, doll, it's like this," said the woman who was probably a man. "The Rainbowers summoned me because they said a fairy fell out of the sky and right on top of our evil Wicked Fairy of the East."

She pointed to Darius' old farmhouse and Darius blinked. At the foundation of the house, near the front steps, he saw two ankles and a pair of the most beautiful pink stilettos he'd ever seen. "How did *that* happen?" Darius asked.

"Listen, doll, you don't have to pretend with me. You dropped that house right on top of that mean old fairy on purpose. And now I'm asking you, are you a good fairy or a bad fairy?"

"Well, I'm not a fairy at all," Darius said. "Fairies aren't real. They're make-believe and they live in story books. I'm just a simple guy from Uranus and this is my dog, Sparky. Have you ever seen Uranus?"

"Honey, I've seen it all."

Darius heard the sound of giggling, as if there were people hiding all around them and listening to them speak. "What's that? Who's laughing?"

The beautiful woman who could have been a man smiled and waved her long fingernails. "Those are the Rainbowers," she said. "And they're laughing because fairies are very real, indeed, doll. I'm a fairy, a good fairy, and that's why they summoned me. My name is

Miss Glitz and I'm the protector of all the Rainbowers here in the Land of Pride."

Darius reached out to shake her large hand and said, "I've never met a real fairy before, especially one as beautiful as you. Can I ask you a question?"

"Of course, doll. You can ask me anything."

"Are you really a man pretending to be a woman? Not that it matters. You're still beautiful. I'm just curious, is all."

"Have you ever heard of drag?"

Darius shook his head.

Miss Glitz laughed and said, "I'm a good fairy who's a drag performer. In other words, I'm a man but I get dressed up as a woman because it's what I love. You can use any pronoun you want with me and I won't get offended. I'm only here to do good work and serve the Rainbowers."

"Okay," Darius said, "I think I'll refer to you as a woman because you're so beautiful."

"Aren't you a sweet little thing," Miss Glitz said.

"May I ask you what Rainbowers are?"

"I'm sorry, doll, I should have known. You don't even know about drag, you poor little helpless thing. How could I expect you to know about Rainbowers. Well, the Rainbowers are all the wonderful dogs who once lived and played on Earth. This is where they come after they pass away. It's not very widely known yet, but someday in the future you'll hear more about it. It's going to become very popular. The dogs cross something called The Rainbow River to get here and they become Rainbowers for all eternity."

Darius glanced down at Sparky and smiled. "Well isn't that wonderful. Did you hear that, Sparky?"

Sparky jumped up and barked.

Miss Glitz lifted her arms and waved them around above her head as if she were about to start dancing.

"Is everything okay?" Darius asked. Every move she made tended to be so dramatic and exaggerated he couldn't tell if she was happy or in distress. "Are you ill?"

She smiled at him, and then started to turn in graceful circles while she repeated two words: "Come out, come out, come out. Come out of your closets and come out of your homes."

While she turned in circles, Darius saw images appear from behind shrubs, trees, houses and walls. They were dogs, but they were all dressed as humans in elaborate costumes that reminded Darius of old-fashioned French paintings he'd seen once in a museum. There were beagles, poodles, bull dogs, and terriers. The males wore velvet waistcoats and the females wore lace-trimmed satin gowns. Dogs acting and behaving as humans suddenly filled the silvery path and started dancing and singing as if they were celebrating something wonderful and magical.

As each one came into view, he noticed every dog breed imaginable, including mixed breeds. They were large and they were small. Some wore hats and others eyeglasses. They moved like dogs and yet they all seemed to have the ability to walk on their hind legs. But more than that, unlike Sparky and all the dogs Darius had ever known, they all had thumbs. Dog thumbs, not human thumbs. But the dog thumbs allowed their paws to function like human hands.

While Darius stood there gaping at them, they started singing and dancing and cheering all around him. A male poodle wearing a black tuxedo jacket took Darius' left hand and a male boxer wearing a red velvet waistcoat took his other hand and they guided him to the center of the silvery path to a large round circle. Miss Glitz, the good fairy, stood on the sidelines watching and smiling with her large hands clasped together and her knees slightly bent as if she were about to curtsy. A cocker spaniel in a pink ruffled dress gave Darius the biggest chocolate bar he'd ever seen in his life, and a sweet little Yorkie wearing a black fedora gave him a bag filled with rainbow colored caramel corn. They seemed to be celebrating something, only Darius had no idea what it was. He kept glancing at Sparky to see how he was reacting to all these animated dogs dancing and singing, but Sparky looked just as confused as he felt.

When they finally settled down and the singing and dancing subsided, a German shepherd wearing a tall black top hat walked up to Darius and said, "We shall now present you with the top honor in our land. You have done the impossible, and we will forever be in your debt." He handed Darius a gold star with the word "Hero" written in the center.

As Darius reached for the star and thanked them for being so kind, there was a puff of yellow and gray smoke on the other side of the silver path and all the Rainbowers ran to the sidelines for cover as if they were terrified for their lives. Everything had seemed so festive and light-hearted a moment earlier and now everyone hid and cowered in small clusters. He remained standing in the middle of the circle, with the gifts of love they'd given him in his arms and the gold hero star in his hand.

An image appeared from the gray and yellow smoke that resembled the heinous, mean-spirited Agnes McCain. It wasn't Agnes McCain, but it could have been her twin sister, and she was wearing a dark brown plaid suit and chunky heeled lace up oxfords with square toes. He'd never seen such a horrible outfit in his life. It was so bad it hurt his feelings. As she glared in his direction and took a few steps closer, she pointed a crooked finger at the house that had fallen on the Wicked Fairy of the East and said, "You killed her."

Miss Glitz walked over to stand beside Darius. "Don't worry, baby, everything will be all right."

"But you said the bad fairy was dead."

"This is her identical twin sister, the Wicked Fairy of the West," said Miss Glitz. "That was the Wicked Fairy of the East. This one is even worse, doll. She's built her entire life on bad spells, too much gin, and a whole shitload of regret."

Well. Darius wasn't sure what to do so he moved closer to Miss Glitz and waited to see what the Wicked Fairy would do. While she shook her crooked finger in his direction, she screamed, "You killed my sister. You'll pay for this."

"I didn't kill anyone," Darius said. He resented her tone. "The house did it."

Sparky barked and growled at this mean fairy version of Agnes McCain.

"It was your house that killed her and you're going to pay for this," said the Wicked Fairy.

At a closer glance Darius noticed that the Wicked Fairy even had the same long crooked nose as Agnes McCain. "It was an accident. My house didn't mean to kill her."

Before the Wicked Fairy could say another word, Miss Glitz said, "Aren't you going to get the pink high-heels, you nasty old hag. They're very special high heels. I know I wouldn't let them go to waste if I were you. And from the looks of it you could use a decent pair of heels, doll." She glanced down at the Wicked Fairy's ugly chunky-heeled Oxfords and scowled.

"The high heels," said the Wicked Fairy. "I have to get them."

She turned and crossed back to the house so she could retrieve her sister's pink glittery high heels. As she bent forward, a puff of pure white smoke appeared and vanished within a matter of seconds. When the clear white smoke was gone, the exposed ankles of the Wicked Fairy's dead sister were all shriveled and decayed and the pink high heels were nowhere to be seen.

The Wicked Fairy turned fast and glared at Miss Glitz. "What did you do with those high heels, you nasty queen?"

Miss Glitz laughed in her face and said, "Doll, I take care of my own." She patted Darius on the back and smiled.

Darius looked down at his feet and noticed that he was now wearing the pink glittery high heels. Even though he had never thought of himself as a woman, he had always wanted a pair of high heels just like this. He never in his life would have had the guts to wear a pair of shoes like this, because in his day and time men weren't allowed to cross gender lines this way. He always thought it would just be a dream and that he'd live out his life fantasizing about wearing shoes like this. Because that's what men like him were expected to do, especially if they wanted to survive.

Then Darius noticed his entire outfit had changed. He'd been wearing the typical homemade beige muslin farm shirt, worn overalls, and boots that most farm boys wore in Uranus. He'd always had one good suit and a good pair of black shoes to his name, and his overalls and boots were his daily outfit. Now he looked down at what he was wearing and he couldn't believe his eyes. Instead of overalls, he was wearing black leather shorts and a black formal Tuxedo jacket. His shirt was pure white and open at the collar, and the entire outfit reminded him of a men's formal tuxedo, with the exception of the short pants and no black bowtie.

He turned to face Miss Glitz and said, "What happened? Why am I dressed this way?"

"Doll, you don't think I'd put you in those adorable high heels wearing those tacky old overalls, do you? Miss Glitz is no amateur, hon. She knows what she's doing, and you have great legs, hon."

The Wicked Fairy turned and glared at Darius' feet. "Give me those shoes this instant. If you don't give them to me I'll destroy this entire Rainbow Village and everyone who lives here.

"Don't you threaten *me*, doll," Miss Glitz said. "You have no power here or over me. I'll turn you into that old tired straight woman who lived in that ugly shoe and you'll have so many kids you really won't know what the fuck to do."

"You wouldn't dare."

Miss Glitz smiled. "You don't wanna find out, doll."

As Miss Glitz lifted her arm slowly, the Wicked Fairy took a step back and her expression filled with fear. But she didn't back down totally. "Give me those shoes. You're not a fairy. You look ridiculous in them and you don't even know how to use them."

Darius glanced down at his feet and checked out the pink glittery high heels again. He kind of liked them. He'd never been the type of man who cared all that much about women's clothing, yet in the same respect he suddenly felt empowered by these shoes for the most unusual reason. Ever since his house had landed in this odd place called the Land of Pride he didn't feel the same social restrictions he'd always felt back in Uranus. He'd always been attracted to other men, which had always made him overly self-conscious about the way he behaved. He'd always taken precautions *not* to appear too effeminate, and he'd always been conscious about the way he carried himself in public. Half the time he didn't even realize he was doing this. It just seemed so natural to hide who he really was. Now that he was in this Land of Pride he didn't feel the same need to self-censor every move and gesture he made, and the high heels he was wearing didn't bother him the same way they would have bothered him back in Uranus. For the first time in his life he felt as if he was expressing himself in a different way, without judgment, shame, or restrictions.

"Don't listen to her, doll," Miss Glitz said. "She knows how powerful those shoes are and she'll do anything to get them. Besides, they look so cute on you."

Darius looked at the shoes again and turned his right foot sideways. "Do you really think so? You don't think they're too much?"

"Oh no, doll, they're fabulous. You've got the legs for them."

"Well you haven't seen the last of me," The Wicked Fairy said. "I'll be watching you, and I'll be watching your dog, too. I'll get those shoes back if it's the last thing I do."

Then the Wicked Fairy took a few steps back and lifted her arms high above her head. She screamed and snapped her fingers 3 times. A second after that, she vanished into a cloud of yellow and gray smoke the same way she'd arrived.

"It's safe to come out again, Rainbowers," said Miss Glitz. "The Wicked Fairy is gone."

While all the Rainbowers gathered around in the town circle, Darius turned to face Miss Glitz and said, "What will I do now? How do I get back to Uranus?"

"You'll have to figure a way out of Pride," Miss Glitz said. "The Wicked Fairy will be plotting and planning to get you now and you won't be safe."

"I'd love to go back to Uranus," Darius said. "I'd love to go back to my family and my life. But I don't know how to do that."

"Well, doll, you are kind of needy and pathetic. You can't fly and you're not a real fairy, so you'll have to walk to the Rainbow City. That's the capital of the Land of Pride. The Queen of Pride lives there and he can help you with Uranus."

Darius tilted his head in confusion. "The Queen of Pride is a *man*?"

"Don't be so serious, doll. Of course he's a man. You really don't know much. It's just a harmless, campy way people like us sometimes refer to each other here in the Land of Pride. King and Queen are gender neutral terms here and they are interchangeable. It's like the way we use the word fairy and the word queer here in

Pride. There's nothing harmful or wrong about either word. We've taken ownership of those words and no one can ever use them against us. Just go with the proverbial flow, so to speak, and never remove those high heels and you'll be just fine. Although, some people still refer to him as the *Wizard* of Pride."

"I think I prefer the Wizard of Pride, if that's okay," Darius said. All this was so new to him it felt as though he was part of a unique culture and he didn't know how to process it all at once. There was so much to learn, and he needed time.

"As long as you're wearing the high heels, you'll have no problems, doll."

"Never remove the high heels? What about when I go to sleep?"

"Never, ever remove the high heels," Miss Glitz said. "You're safe from the Wicked Fairy as long as you're wearing them."

Darius took a few steps forward and turned all the way around to face Miss Glitz. "Which way is this Rainbow City? How do I get there?"

The sparkling crystal chandelier appeared again and Miss Glitz hopped up and sat on one of the arms. She pointed and said, "Follow the silvery gilded road, doll. It will lead you directly to the Rainbow City where you'll find The Wizard of Pride."

As Darius was about to ask another question, Miss Glitz smiled and the crystal chandelier began to rise quickly. It floated up into the sky and it grew smaller and smaller until it couldn't be seen anymore. All the Rainbowers, all breeds and genders, jumped up and down and their fancy clothes and cheered Miss Glitz's departure as if they were bidding farewell to a goddess. While everyone cheered, two others handed Darius a purple satchel so he could carry the gifts they'd given him.

When Miss Glitz was nowhere to be seen, a tall black poodle Rainbower wearing a royal blue velvet jacket and a large royal blue hat with a huge white plume walked over to Darius and said, "Just follow the silvery gilded path."

After he said that, the rest of the Rainbowers began to repeat it in unison. Darius and sparky took a few steps forward and began their journey to the Rainbow City to search for the Wizard of Pride. He had no idea where he was going and he didn't stop to think about it for too long. He didn't have any choice. If he didn't find the all-powerful and all-knowing Wizard of Pride he'd never get back to Uranus and see the people he loved the most again. He did find one thing interesting, though. The pink glittery high heels were the most comfortable walking shoes he'd ever worn, it was as though he was walking on marshmallows.. In spite of his concerns about wearing such tall stilettos, he didn't stumble or stagger once, and it felt so perfectly natural to him.

Chapter Seven

Darius and Sparky traveled down the silver path until they reached a curvy fork in the road without any signs pointing in any directions. Darius glanced down at Sparky and said, "Now what do we do?"

Sparky looked up and barked.

"I'm afraid we're just going to have to guess which way to go and hope for the best, Sparky."

Both roads were silvery with glitter, both led in two different directions, and both appeared to be identical. Darius glanced back and forth at each road and wondered for a moment, and then he heard a noise coming from an area to his right with dense shrubs. It sounded like a whistle, but he wasn't certain. So he took a few steps toward the shrubs and said, "Is someone in there? Who's in those bushes? I demand you come out now."

"I'm not ready to come out. Coming out is not an option for men like me. If I were ready to come out I wouldn't have any problems at all. Coming out isn't easy for some of us. Coming out is a *huge* decision. It can be very traumatic. Stop forcing me."

"I don't care," Darius said. "Come out where I can see you this minute."

There was a second or two of silence, and then a deep voice said, "I'm thinking."

Sparky barked again and Darius tilted his head sideways. "Who's there? Come out so I can see you. I could use a little help. I'm trying to figure out which way to go." Even though this was a complete stranger, Darius was thrilled not to be alone anymore.

The thick shrubs moved and a tall figure crossed through an opening. He stood about six feet tall, he had a heavy reddish beard, and wore overalls and boots just like the farm boys Darius had grown up with. Only this guy wasn't wearing a shirt; just overalls and boots. Darius couldn't help but notice the bulging muscles in his arms and chest, not to mention the way the tight overalls pulled across his crotch. This man definitely made Darius' heart beat a little faster, in a very erotic way.

He stopped and looked Darius up and down and said, "That sure is an unusual outfit, and I've never seen a guy wear shoes like that."

Darius didn't appreciate his tone. "Do you have a problem with what I'm wearing?"

He threw his large hands forward and said, "Oh, no. It's not that. You look just fine. In fact, you look better than fine. I just never saw anything like that where I come from. It's just different, is all."

"Well, to be honest I'm not used to wearing shoes like this either. I never thought I would be wearing high heels."

The guy looked up at the blue sky for a moment and tapped his chin. "I'm not sure where I come from. I'm not even sure who I am. That's my problem. I don't know who I am. All I know is that I'm different from other guys. I'm not like them at all. You're the first person I've ever told this to, but I'm not at all attracted to women. I'd rather be with men. Sorry if I offend you, but I see no point in lying. You seem like a person I can trust."

"Well you didn't offend me at all," Darius said. "I understand completely. I'm not attracted to women either. That's how I wound up here. This mean old woman named Agnes McCain threatened to tell everyone she caught me naked with one of the farm hands if I didn't give her my dog, Sparky. This is Sparky."

The tall man with the big muscles smiled at Sparky and said, "It's nice to meet you." He looked at Darius and shrugged. "I wish I could tell you my name, but as I said, I'm not even sure who I am. Do you know who you are?"

Darius sent him a smile. "Well my name is Darius and I come from a small town called Uranus. I grew up on a farm and my aunt and uncle raised me. I know who I am. I've always known. I just never let anyone know who I am. And I have to find a way to get back to Uranus."

"It's nice to meet you, Darius," he said. "I wish I could tell you my name. But the only thing I know about myself is that I'm attracted to other men and I've never actually been with another man. I don't even think I'm from around here. It's all so strange to me, this land of rainbows. Oh, how I wish I could figure it all out. Maybe you can help me. I'm afraid I'm not very strong."

Darius had to admit he found this guy attractive, and the fact that he'd never been with a man brought out all of Darius' basic instincts. He reached out and squeezed this guy's bicep and said, "I think we should call you Strong Man for now. I think that name fits you perfectly."

"Strong Man?"

"Oh, of course," Darius said. "You're so big and strong and handsome. Until you figure out who you are, it's the perfect name for you."

"I never thought of myself as strong. Do you really think I'm strong?"

"Of course I do. Why you're one of the strongest men I've ever met."

"You're too kind, Darius."

While they were talking, and while Darius was rubbing Strong Man's bicep, he'd grown fully erect. When Darius glanced down at his crotch he saw the outline of a huge, thick cock ready to burst out of his overalls. So he reached down between Strong Man's legs and grabbed his erection gently. He sent him a naughty smile and asked, "What on Earth is *this*?"

Strong Man's face turned red and he began to stutter. "You see what I mean. I'm not normal. I'm not like other guys. All I want to do right now is throw you down in the bushes and rip off your clothes. I'm sorry. I'm terrible."

"Oh no," Darius said. "Please don't be sorry. There's nothing wrong with you and there's nothing to apologize about. I think you're perfectly normal, at least according to my standards."

"You do?"

Darius squeezed strong man's erection harder and said, "Take me into those bushes and show me what's inside there."

Strong Man squared his shoulders and lifted his head a little higher. "I can take you there. It's just a grassy private area. It's nothing special. Shouldn't these things happen in somewhere special?"

"Then we'll make it special."

Even though Darius wanted to get back to Uranus, he figured a slight diversion couldn't hurt. After all, he was in the Land of Pride where everything seemed to be normal and okay. He didn't think anyone would judge him if he fooled around with a good-looking young guy in overalls. Evidently, Strong Man seemed to need an ego boost, and Darius felt obligated to help him out.

Darius reached out for Strong Man's hand and Strong Man led him back to the bushes. Darius told Sparky to stay on the silver path and wait for him, and he knew Sparky would listen. They passed through an open section and wound up in a small grassy area that was completely secluded from the silver path. The moment they were out of sight, Darius reached into Strong Man's overalls and started stroking one of the biggest, firmest erections he'd ever held in his hand.

"How does that feel?" Darius asked.

Strong Man sighed and said, "It feels wonderful. You're wonderful. It's just that I've never done anything like this with another man and I'm not sure what to do. I don't want to disappoint you. Oh, I'm such a waste of human flesh. I can't do anything right."

"Please don't say that," Darius said. "You're a big strong good looking man and I'm going to do everything. You'll learn in time. But for right now you just stand there and let me do all the work. You have nothing to worry about."

Without even waiting for Strong Man to reply, Darius pulled his hand out of Strong Man's overalls and he took a step back. While Strong Man watched, Darius removed the black tuxedo jacket, the shirt, and then he removed the black leather short pants. He wasn't wearing underwear and he was naked within seconds. The only clothing on his body was the pink glittery stilettos. He looked into Strong Man's deep blue eyes and said, "I'm sorry but I can't remove the shoes. They are some kind of magic shoes and if I remove them I could get into a lot of trouble. I hope that's okay."

Strong Man had been biting his lip. "They're fine. You're a very good-looking guy. Can I touch you? I've never touched a man before."

Darius smiled. "Of course you can touch me. You can touch me anywhere you want."

Strong Man lifted his hands and rested them on Darius' naked waist, and then he slid them down Darius' hips and around his buttocks a few times. "Your skin is very soft, but it's firm, too. This is nice. You make me feel so safe."

Darius took a few steps toward him and said, "It's very nice. I think you're very good looking, too. And now I'm going to show you. I just want you to stand there and do nothing. Let me do all the work. I think you'll like it."

They were standing outside, but totally secluded from the road. The grass was like no other grass Darius had ever seen before. It was thick and deep green and soft. It resembled a carpet and he slowly went down on his knees. He looked up at Strong Man and said, "Unbutton your overalls."

Strong Man seemed so excited by then Darius could have told him to do anything and he would have responded. He quickly unfastened all the buttons on his overalls and Darius pulled them down his body

66

slowly. His body was just as nice as Darius had imagined it would be. He was all man, solid, with hair in all the right places and that nice thick cock. And he had no idea he was this magnificently attractive.

Darius wanted Strong Man's first time to be a wonderful memory, so he moved slowly and gently, without any sudden moves or awkward gestures. He pressed his palms on Strong Man's solid thighs and moved forward so he could rest his mouth between Strong Man's legs. He started sucking and licking gently, between Strong Man's balls and thighs while he ran his fingers up and down his legs. The taste and feel and smell of a man was pure enjoyment for Darius and he was enjoying this as much as Strong Man. He wanted to remain submissive and gentle because he knew Strong Man wasn't ready for anything that required more thought at that moment.

After he finished sucking and licking Strong Man's balls, he opened his mouth and gently sucked his dick all the way into his mouth. This was something Darius had learned to do well thanks to the guys who worked on his farm. When he'd first started sucking their dicks it had been awkward and it took some time to perfect his technique. However, Darius learned quickly and he now knew how to take a man all the way to the back of his throat without gagging or choking once. He didn't make those vulgar awkward moves by haplessly jerking his head all over the place and making the guy flinch with his teeth. He sucked the entire dick into his mouth, pressed his tongue to the base of the dick, and he didn't stop sucking until that dick in his mouth exploded.

It happened quickly with Strong Man that day,

which didn't surprise Darius in the least. He'd expected it, because he'd been sucking extra hard to really make the first experience more memorable. Darius felt Strong Man's dick swell in his mouth, and he felt Strong Man's legs begin to shudder. He started breathing heavier and he reached down and grabbed both sides of Darius' head and said, "Oh, I can't hold back."

Darius looked up at him with innocent eyes and nodded to let him know it was okay.

A minute later, Strong Man came and his entire body shuddered. He held Darius' head in both hands and pushed his pelvis toward Darius' face and grunted a few times. Darius continued to suck with the same intensity and he didn't move once. He sucked until he knew it was time for him to reach down and grab his own dick so he could come, too.

A few minutes after that, Darius reached down to pick up his black leather shorts and Strong Man rested his palm on Darius' bottom. He patted his bottom a few times and said, "That was amazing. Thank you."

Darius turned and kissed his hairy chest. "I'm glad you liked it. You deserved it."

"You're so nice," Strong Man said. "I'm not used to that. I'm only used to feeling guilty and hating myself. The self-loathing never ends. I never thought I'd meet anyone that would make me feel good about being this way."

"I know exactly what you mean," Darius said, as he leaned on Strong Man to put on his pants. "I've felt the same way, trust me. Maybe someday they will come up with a word for men like us, a good word and not something that's an offensive insult." Of course he'd heard the word homosexual and he'd always despised it.

"They do have words for men like us, but I don't like them very much, especially the word homosexual. It makes me feel like a science experiment."

"I know what you mean. I never liked the word homosexual much either. I'm talking about a word for men like us that's positive and, I don't know, gay. It should be a gay, fun happy word."

"I'd like that," Strong Man said. "But for right now I'd just like to figure out who I am and where I belong. I don't have a clue."

Darius pulled up his pants and turned to face him. He put his arms around his shoulders and caressed the back of his neck. Darius had never been able to do this with a man after sex, especially not out in the open this way. He'd always felt the need to be discreet and cautious so that no one would ever suspect anything about him. This meant that showing any signs of affection toward another man before or after sex had always been off limits. For a change, even if it wouldn't last forever, it was nice to just put his arms around a man's shoulders and caress his neck in a purely affectionate way. He'd seen women do this to men in movies all the time, but he'd never seen a man d o this to another man, in a natural, harmless way.

"You should come with us," Darius said. "We're going to the Rainbow City to find the Wizard of Pride. He knows everything and he'll be able to help you figure out who you are."

"Do you think so?" Strong Man asked. He started squeezing Darius' bottom, as if he couldn't get enough of it.

Darius didn't mind. He had a feeling now that Strong Man had had his first sexual encounter with another man he would want more of it. "I've heard the Wizard of Pride can do anything."

"Okay," Strong Man said, with a great big smile. "I'll go. After all, I'll never find out who I am unless I try."

They finished getting dressed and Strong Man escorted Darius out of the bushes with his palm pressed firmly to Darius' back. Darius knew this wasn't the love of his life, but he was happy to have found him. As strong as he appeared, Strong Man was just as terrified deep down inside as any other man who was like them. If nothing else, they could help each other and support each other in this strange land called Pride, and maybe even have a little happy fun while they were doing this.

Chapter Eight

Darius and Strong Man traveled down the silver path until they reached a tree-lined area that made them both stop and gaze. The trees didn't resemble any of the trees Darius had known back in Uranus. They were different from the trees he'd seen in Pride so far, too. These trees had an exotic, tropical appeal, with rough flakey trunks and unusually wide green leaves. As Darius took a few steps closer to one of these trees he glanced upward and noticed they were fruit trees. His favorite kind of fruit tree.

Darius pointed up at one of the trees and said, "Oh, look. They're banana trees, Strong Man. And they are the biggest, thickest, juiciest bananas I think I've ever seen. I just love a nice big banana."

"They're huge," said Strong Man.

When Darius turned to look at another banana tree, he felt something poke him in the buttocks and someone with a deep wrecked voice said, "You like banana, baby?"

Darius turned fast but he didn't see anyone standing there. He knew it wasn't Strong Man speaking because he was still standing with Sparky on the silver path. He turned again to see if anyone was behind him and he felt another poke in the buttocks and this time someone said, "Nice ass, baby. I'd like to hit that."

This time he turned around faster and caught the banana tree moving, as if it were human. And there was a round wrinkly section of the banana tree trunk facing Darius that resembled a mouth with lips. This time the lips moved and the tree said, "You like banana? I've got a nice big one for you, baby."

Although Darius knew trees weren't supposed to speak, he figured anything could happen in Pride and he said, "I love bananas. May I have one?"

The banana tree giggled and said, "Oh, I've got a nice big one for you. Take off your pants."

Before Darius could reply, Strong Man stormed over to where Darius was standing and he shook his finger at the banana tree. "See here, you have no right to speak to him that way. He's not from around here and there's no need to be rude. Darius is a gentleman, which is more than I can say for you and your sour green bananas."

"It's okay," Darius said. "I'm not offended, Strong Man. I do like a banana."

The banana tree poked Strong Man in the shoulder with a big ripe banana and said, "I'll have you know I have the best and biggest bananas in Pride. They are not sour or green."

Strong Man squared his shoulders. "Oh yeah, well you don't have any manners that's for sure."

Darius had a feeling this exchange would continue to devolve, so he grabbed Strong Man's arm and said, "Let's go. I don't need a banana today. I'm fine."

The banana tree laughed again and said, "That's a shame. You'd love *my* banana."

"That's it," Strong Man said. "I've had enough of this rude tree and his sexual harassment. I'm going to make sour banana *bread* out of him."

Darius pulled Strong Man's arm harder and said, "Let's go. I want to get out of here now." He didn't want to see any trouble. He was thrilled to have found someone to walk with him and he didn't want that to change.

Even though Strong Man turned to follow Darius back to the road, he sent the rude old banana tree a backward glance and said, "I'll bet those sour green bananas taste just as bad as they look anyway. We're better off without them."

As they trailed off toward the road, the banana tree began to shout. "How dare you insult my bananas."

They started running because the tree began to throw bananas at them, big, thick, juicy bananas, too. They grabbed a few bananas that flew in their direction and put them in the purple satchel the Rainbowers had given Darius, and then they went off in two different directions without even realizing it. Darius noticed one particularly large banana on the side of the silver path and he went down on his knees and crossed through a few bushes to get it. However, as he reached for this extra-large, thick banana on the grass, still on his hands and knees, he noticed a large pair of thick black leather boots and he gulped.

A deep throaty voice said, "Who are you and what are you doing here?"

Darius didn't know where Sparky and Strong Man were. He glanced up slowly and found a tall, stocky muscular man glaring down at him, with his hairy arms folded across his chest and a scowl on his rugged face. He had a thick dark beard, but not as reddish as Strong Man's beard. He wore the most unusual outfit, which would have been out of place in almost any setting other than Pride. The outfit was all black leather: skin tight black chaps that exposed his tight white underwear, a tight black leather vest that exposed his bare muscular chest, and two black leather arm bands across each bulging bicep. Once when the traveling circus had passed through Uranus, Darius had seen rough looking men on motorcycles dressed this way and he'd been fascinated by them.

Darius looked up and smiled. "I'm Darius. I'm on my way to see the Wizard of Pride. I'm sorry if I bothered you. I just want to get my banana and I'll leave you alone. My friend, Strong Man, and my dog, Sparky, are waiting for me on the silver path."

The man in leather laughed and said, "I'd like to watch you eat that big banana very, very slowly."

As the man in leather said this, Strong Man and Sparky walked up to where Darius was still kneeling and Strong Man said, "Hey, watch your mouth. This is a gentleman you're talking to."

"You watch *your* mouth," the leather man said. "You don't even look like you know who you are."

Strong Man squared his shoulders and looked him in the eye. "Well I'm on my way to Rainbow City to see the Wizard of Pride to find out who I am. And there's no need to be rude."

Darius stood up and frowned. "You really are a very rude man, if I do say so myself. We're only passing through and we didn't mean any harm at all. We've done nothing to offend you."

The man in leather frowned and looked down at

his boots. "I'm sorry. I can't help it. I am rude. I'm angry and I hate myself. I hate being who I am and yet I can't help being who I am. I'm just one big self-loathing mess and there's nothing I can do about it."

Well now Darius felt a little sorry for him. He reached out and caressed his bicep and said, "It's okay. We all have something wrong with us. I'm trying to find my way back to Uranus and Strong Man wants to find out who he is. Maybe you should come with us to Rainbow City and talk to the Wizard of Pride. He might be able to help you with all that self-loathing and self-hatred."

Strong Man smiled. "I think Darius is right. You should come with us. After all, we all have one thing in common. We're all attracted to men."

"What's your name?" Darius asked.

"They call me Butch," he said. "That's because I tend to over compensate by being overly masculine. I'm so masculine sometimes it's toxic."

"Well you don't have to be that way," Darius said. "It's not like anyone is forcing you to be that way."

"I know," Butch said. "I can't help it. People are mean. When I was a kid in school I was carrying my books the wrong way and everyone started to tease me. They said I was carrying my books like a girl and they started calling me names like fairy and queer. So I vowed from that day on I would never let anyone treat me that way again. Now it's become a way of life and I can't seem to change it no matter how hard I try."

"Well there's nothing wrong with being mas-culine," Darius said. "I think you're very attractive, but you don't have to be rude about it." Darius had always been extremely attracted to men who tended to be more dominant and forceful. It's not that he found rude, obnoxious men attractive. This was different and it had to be in the right context. On a day-to-day basis he didn't care for obnoxious behavior, but when he was intimate with a man he didn't mind being dominated and bossed around a little.

As if he could read Darius' mind, Butch looked him up and down and grabbed his arm hard. "I think you're very attractive, too. You wanna lick my boots?"

The instant Butch grabbed his arm Darius felt the beginning of an erection and his heart began to race.

"Hey, let go of him," Strong Man said. "And stop saying vulgar things like that."

"Now, wait a second, Strong Man," Darius said. "Let's not get too upset. He's not hurting me. It's okay." He wanted this tall dark man in black leather to hold him and yank him around a little. His heart was racing so fast by then he wanted to rip off his clothes and straddle Butch's waist.

Strong Man smiled and said, "Oh, I see. You know what? Sparky and I will just go over to the other side of the road and leave you two alone for a few minutes. We'll sit under a tree and share a banana."

Butch was still holding Darius' arm and Darius was looking into Butch's eyes. Darius nodded and said, "Okay, Strong Man. You go rest. This shouldn't take long."

When Strong Man and Sparky were gone, Butch pulled Darius closer and said, "You don't seem effeminate and yet you're wearing those pink high heels. What's up with that?"

"Do you have to label everything?" Darius asked. He was fully erect now and his chest was heaving.

"Why does everything always have to be so gender specific? Can't I just wear shoes and leave it at that?"

"Don't get me wrong. I like the way you're dressed. I'm a top, a total top. I never bottom."

Even though Darius had always considered himself versatile in the sense that he could either be a top or a bottom during sex, he always seemed to attract men who were only tops. He didn't mind, especially not with Butch. He'd never been with a man this dominant, this unusual, or this honest. Even though this guy's brand of honesty could be somewhat abrupt, it was refreshing to know that Butch wasn't lying to him about anything.

"That's okay," Darius said. "I don't mind in the least if you're a top." Then he looked even deeper into his eyes. He wanted to show him how submissive he could be. "I like that."

"I bet you do," Butch said, as if he could read Darius' mind. He took another step forward and grabbed the back of Darius' neck. "Get naked, but leave the shoes on."

"Is it safe here?" Darius asked. He was so accustomed to being on guard at all times back on the farm in Uranus, he couldn't shake the feeling that someone would catch him having sex with a man.

"That's one thing about being in Pride you don't have to worry about," Butch said. "From what I've been told, no one judges and we're all equal. You're safe."

It took Darius less than a minute to strip off his clothes and lean up against Butch. He liked the way the warm black leather felt against his naked skin. He ran his palms up and down Butch's hairy chest and licked his nipples. Darius had always loved sex with men but this was different because Butch was that rare man who exuded dominance with every move he made and he wasn't even aware of it. He smelled like a man, he spoke like a man, and most of all he tasted like a man.

As they stood there in the grass, with nothing but trees and shrubs around them, Darius ran his fingers up the back of Butch's head, through his thick dark hair, and said, "What do you want me to do for you?"

Butch reached around and slapped his naked butt in a playful way and said, "Call me Sir."

"Yes, Sir."

He slapped him again and said, "I didn't hear that."

Darius spoke louder. "Yes, Sir."

He slapped him twice and said, "That's better. Now get down on your knees and suck my dick. And don't stop until I tell you to stop."

Darius kissed his chest and said, "Yes, Sir."

He went down on his knees and pulled Butch's erection out of his white underwear. It wasn't difficult to do because he was wearing those black leather chaps that were open in the front and back. The moment he had Butch's dick in his hands he wrapped his lips around the head and started sucking slowly. He was one of those men who pre-come immediately, which made sucking his dick even more pleasurable.

A few minutes later, Butch grabbed Darius by the hair and yanked his head back a little. "Tell me what you really want now."

Darius licked some pre-come from the tip of his erection and glanced up at him. "Fuck me, Sir."

"I didn't hear that."

He lifted his voice. "Fuck me, Sir. Please, Sir. Fuck me with that huge dick."

"Stand up and turn around," Butch said.

Darius followed his order and Butch grabbed him by the waist with one hand and by the throat with the other. As Darius spread his legs and arched his back, Butch squeezed his neck even harder. Then he released his waist and slapped his ass again. "Tell me what you want, louder."

"Fuck me, Sir. Fuck me as hard as you can, Sir."

Butch lubricated his erection with his own saliva and then he shoved it deep into Darius' body without hesitating. Of course it was so sudden it hurt a little at first but Darius was no virgin and Butch seemed to know this. Darius knew the pain would eventually subside and he encouraged Butch by spreading his legs even wider. He was the first man Darius had ever known who was this aggressive, dominant and competent. He wasn't worried about hurting Darius because he seemed to know instinctively that this is what Darius wanted from him. He seemed to know what would please Darius the most and he didn't hold back from giving it to him.

They remained in this position the entire time, with Darius standing in front of him and Butch fucking Darius from behind. Butch didn't release his neck once, and he fucked him so hard at one point he lifted him up off the grass. They reached a point where everything went completely blank and the only sound that could be heard was Butch's pelvis slamming into Darius' buttocks. With every ounce of control Darius lost, he grew closer to climax. He wasn't touching his own erection either. His climax began to build from a place deep in his body each time Butch pushed into him. And right before they both reached climax simultaneously, Butch whispered into his ear and said, "What do you want now?"

"Come inside me, Sir," Darius said with a wrecked voice. "Come inside me, please, Sir."

And that's exactly what he did. A moment later, Butch grunted and his entire body went still. He pushed his erection so deeply into Darius' body that he lifted Darius up off the grass again and Darius experienced multiple orgasms this time. It wasn't just the physical act of getting fucked this hard that made Darius climax this way. It was the emotional and psychological images of what they were doing that actually brought Darius off. For Darius it was always more about the thought of what he was doing with a man than the actual physical act he was performing.

When it was over, they both remained still for a moment and Butch released Darius' neck. "Damn I needed that."

Darius leaned back and turned his head so he could kiss him. "So did I."

By the time Darius was dressed and ready to join Strong Man and Sparky, Butch seemed eager to accompany them to Rainbow City to see if he could figure out a way to solve his problem. He said something interesting to Darius that made Darius stop and think about his entire existence as a man who loved other men. While they were heading back to the silver path, he put his palm on the small of Darius' back and said, "You know, I think we're more than just this. We're more than just sex. There's something that goes a lot deeper with men like us that no one ever seems to notice. I just want to figure out a way to be okay with that, and to not hate what I am. And I am willing to give anything a try, because anything has to be better than the way I feel about myself right now."

At that moment, in the middle of nowhere in a place that Darius wasn't even sure existed, he knew exactly what Butch meant, because he'd felt that way himself more than once himself.

Chapter Nine

As the sun in Pride began to set over the horizon, Darius, Strong Man, Butch, and Sparky grew quiet. They'd been walking for a long time without stopping and now that it was getting darker they all seemed less animated than earlier that day. Darius didn't want to admit that he was starting to get a little flutter in his stomach at the prospect of what might be out there in all that vast darkness. He wasn't sure how the others felt and he didn't want them to be as worried as he was.

When it was almost dark, Strong Man said, "Does anyone know if there are creatures in Pride?"

Darius blinked. "What kind of creatures?"

Strong Man shrugged. "You know, like wild animals. These woods could be filled with coyotes, wildcats, and bears."

"Bears?" Darius asked. He'd never actually seen a bear.

Butch must have been thinking along the same lines. "Of course there are bears in these woods. There are all kinds of wild animals. I wouldn't be shocked to see a lion or a tiger, but most likely it will be a bear. A big fuzzy, hairy bear."

As they continued walking, Darius said, "Oh that's ridiculous. We're not in the jungle. We're in a place called Pride, where chocolate grows on trees and cotton candy grows on bushes. I bet there isn't a lion, or even a bear, anywhere within miles from here."

They heard a noise in the woods that sounded as if something was walking on dried twigs and Darius reached out to hold Butch's large hand. The noise grew louder and even Sparky lifted his head and started sniffing the air. Strong Man grabbed Darius' other hand and squeezed it so tightly Darius made a face.

Then the noise sounded as if it was getting closer and something huge and hairy and dark jumped out of the darkness onto the silver path and said, "Sure there are bears. There are plenty of bears around here. I'm living proof." Whatever this creature was growled and lunged at Sparky and poor Sparky ran behind the three of them and whimpered.

Darius yanked his hands free from the others, took a step forward and shook his finger at this creature. No one threatened his dog, not Agnes McCain and certainly not some idiot in the woods. The minute Darius saw Sparky cower he went into attack mode and as he shook his finger he said, "Don't you dare threaten *my* dog, you big bully. Pick on someone your own size." Of course after he said this he realized that none of them actually were bigger than this creature. But he couldn't help himself. He had to protect his dog. Sparky was all he had left in the world.

"Oh yeah," said the large, dark figure. "We'll see about that, won't we?"

Darius would not back down to bullies. He'd been bullied before as a child and he'd learned the best way to deal with them was to go right back at them. So he took another step forward and this time he got a better look at the large figure. At first he gasped, and then he said, "Why you're not a real bear at all. You're just a big hairy man who likes to go around scaring poor helpless dogs and people."

"Well, I could be a bear," the large figure said. The faster he spoke the more pronounced his lisp became, and he had a strong southern accent. "I could be just as bold and aggressive as *him*." He pointed to Butch and shook his finger.

Butch smiled. "Not on your best day, sweetie. Get over yourself. You're about as aggressive and bold as my grandmother."

"Oh, dear," the large figure said. He lifted his right arm and let his wrist dangle in such an obvious way Darius felt like hugging him. "I'll never be anything but a sissy, a limp-wristed, effeminate lisping sissy boy. It's no use. Go ahead, pick on me and call me names. I'm used to being treated that way by everyone. It's my fate in life."

As this poor soul sat down on a rock, Darius walked over to him and set his palm on his broad shoulder. "We didn't mean to hurt your feelings. Really, we didn't. We're very sorry if we've offended you in any way. But you're the one who tried to attack and frighten us. We were only protecting ourselves. You were big and frightening for a moment or two."

The large figure glanced up at him and smiled. "I was? I actually frightened you for a moment or two?"

Darius sent the other two a look and winked. Then he glanced back at the large figure and said, "Of course you did. You can be very intimidating when you want to be."

Butch had picked up on Darius' signal and he nodded. "Yeah, you scared the crap out of me."

"Me, too," said Strong Man.

The large figure crossed his feet at the ankle and waved a limp wrist in their direction. With a lisp that became even more obvious, he said, "Oh, you're just saying that to make me feel better. I've heard that before, too. I either get praise or I get pity. I'm a mess." Then he lowered his head and started to cry.

"Oh dear," Darius said. He looked at Butch and Strong Man for support. "Please don't cry. We really didn't mean to hurt your feelings. We're not perfect ourselves. I'm Darius and you see, I have these urges that I can't seem to control sometimes. I like men. I like all kinds of men. I've only known these two guys for a short time and I've already slept with both of them. And all I really want is to fall in love and be with one man for the rest of my life, but I'm starting to think that will never happen."

Strong Man said, "That's true. Darius will spread his legs for anyone. You should have seen what he did with Butch. I'm amazed he can still walk."

Darius sent him a sideways glance and said, "I don't need help here, thanks."

"Oops, sorry," said Strong Man. "No offense."

The large effeminate figure lifted both arms and both wrists went limp and he said, "So you're telling me that you're a slut, honey?"

Darius had never liked that word, but he couldn't deny it either. "Well, I guess I am, sometimes. I'm not always sure who I am. And Butch here is too aggressive and he's not happy about being who he is. He hates himself and he wants to be just like other men out there and he doesn't want to be attracted to men. In fact, his self-loathing runs so deep he's in denial more than half the time. And this guy here is Strong Man. He doesn't even know who he is, the poor guy. So you see we're all flawed in one way or another, and now we're heading to Rainbow City to see the Wizard of Pride. We're hoping he'll be able to help us, especially me because I want to get back to Uranus."

The dark figure blinked. "My *what*?"

Darius nodded. "That's where I come from, a town called Uranus."

He glanced down at Darius' pink high heels and said, "Well Uranus must be a lot of fun, honey, because I sure do love your shoes. I'd like a pair in size 14."

Darius extended his hand and said. "I'm Darius, and these are my friends, Strong Man and Butch. This is my dog, Sparky. It's very nice to meet you."

He stood up and shook Darius' hand and said, "You can call me, Teddy. That's what all my good friends call me because I remind them of a big furry Teddy Bear." When he said the name Teddy, with his thick southern accent, it sounded more like *Tay-dee*.

After they all exchanged the basic pleasantries, Butch grew serious and his voice went lower. "Well, we should be going. It's late and we have a long way."

Darius had an idea. "You should come with us, Teddy. Maybe the Wizard of Pride could help you, too."

Teddy thought for a moment, and then he turned and almost curtsied. "Do you really think so?"

Darius nodded. "According to Miss Glitz, the Good Fairy, the Wizard of Pride is all powerful and all-knowing and he can do anything."

Teddy put his hands on his hips and cocked his head sideways. "Well you know what, honey, it might be worth a try. If the Wizard of Pride can turn me into a real man so I won't be sissy anymore, I'll do anything. I just want to be normal. Let's roll."

* * *

They walked for a few more hours until they stumbled across the most adorable little cottage Darius had ever seen. It reminded him of a cottage he'd seen in a storybook once. It was a two-story Cape Cod built out of stone that had been whitewashed in all the right places. The mullioned windows were trimmed in white, the front door was pale lavender, and the roof had light gray shingles. It was surrounded by a whitewashed picket fence, with a garden that had flowers from every color in the rainbow. Every shrub had been pruned into a perfectly neat round and the front walk had been constructed out of golden bricks. And best of all, the entire place was illuminated with well-planned lighting.

There was a sign on the front gate with a small spotlight and Darius said, "Let's go read it and see what it says. Maybe whoever lives there will let us rest for the night."

"Oh, sweetie," said Teddy. "That would be nice. Her feet are really starting to kill her." Teddy tended to refer to himself in the third person every once in a while, with feminine pronouns, and he didn't even realize he was doing this.

They all walked up to the gate and Darius leaned forward to read the sign. "Guest Cottage. Everyone is welcome and no one will be turned away. Please leave it as you found it."

Butch shrugged. "Well I guess that means we can rest here for the night." He placed his palm on Darius' buttocks and squeezed it.

"I know I could use a rest," said Strong Man. He winked at Darius.

Teddy looked at Darius and said, "Your feet must be killing you, honey, in those high heels." He seemed fascinated with the pink stilettos. He kept looking at them as if he wanted to snatch them from Darius' feet.

Darius shrugged. "Actually, not really. I've never worn a more comfortable pair of shoes. But I could use a rest, and I think Sparky could use a rest as well. Let's go inside and see what it's like."

Sparky barked, and Darius opened the gate. As they crossed to the golden brick path and headed toward the lavender front door, they glanced around at the colorful flowers and perfect shrubs without saying a word.

Butch opened the front door first and he guided Darius into the house with his palm. Butch couldn't help taking control this way and Darius didn't really mind. He'd been thinking about the way Butch had fucked him earlier and he was starting to wonder when they would do it again. He'd also been thinking about Strong Man's nice dick and he was hoping they wouldn't mind doing a three-way before they reached the Rainbow City. He wasn't really attracted to Teddy, and he had a feeling… instinct… that Teddy wasn't attracted to him either. But he didn't mind in the least if Teddy watched as long as Teddy didn't mind.

The main floor of the cottage appeared to be one large open living space, with a small country kitchen to the left, a dedicated dining area next to that, and a larger great room to the right with an impressive walk-in white-washed stone fireplace. The wooden floors had been hand-painted to resemble a pale gray and white checkerboard, the walls were chalky white, and there were pecan colored beams above their heads. Even the over stuffed upholstered furniture had been covered in several different shades of white. However, one thing was odd. It wasn't a two-story house after all. The cottage only had one floor and rustic crossbeams supported the two-story ceiling. The only sleeping area in the small house seemed to be a dedicated space toward the back with one full sized, white hand-painted bed, two white hand-painted night stands, and an intricate weather-beaten old trunk at the foot of the bed.

"Oh no," Darius said. "There are four of us and only one full size bed."

Teddy must have noticed that Strong Man and Butch had been reaching around to grab Darius' butt. Teddy hadn't made one move toward Darius and that wasn't a surprise to anyone. He waved his wrist and said, "Don't worry about me, girls. I'll take the sofa. I prefer to sleep alone and I'm not in the least interested in any of *that* sort of thing." He glanced down at the way Butch was patting Darius' butt and laughed.

Strong Man sent him a look and said, "You're not interested in sex at all?"

"I didn't say that, honey," Teddy said. "It's just that I prefer big men, big hairy men with lots of fur and great big happy smiles. I like men with big titties. Nothing personal, but none of you really do it for me." When he said titties, he pronounced it *tayt-tees*.

"I understand that perfectly," Darius said.

"I guess I understand, too," said Strong Man.

"Well I'll fuck anything," Butch said, with a deep, loud voice and a great big smile. He sent Teddy a wink.

Teddy jumped back and put his left hand on his hip. "Well, sweetie, keep dreaming." He started referring to himself in the third person again. "She does not sleep around with just anyone. She has rules about that sort of thing, and a strict personal code of ethics."

"Stop that, Butch," Darius said. "Leave Teddy alone. I admire him and I wish I could be more like him sometimes. It's just that I get these urges and they're so strong. I need a man, or two, on a regular basis otherwise I have trouble sleeping. And frankly, I can't even explain this to myself most of the time."

Chapter Ten

They found an ice box in the cottage's country kitchen that had been stocked with food, as if the little whitewashed cottage had been waiting for them to arrive. The whitewashed farm house dining table had been set for four people, with plates, utensils, and a white linen table cloth and matching napkins. Everything in the icebox had been set in the most adorable wicker baskets lined with red and white-checkered cloths. It was the perfect cold supper and all they had to do was sit down at the table and eat. The fried chicken was still crispy and tender, the potato salad thick and creamy, and the rolls were so light and delicate they practically floated off their plates. As if that wasn't enough, they finished their meal with lemon meringue pie so tall and fluffy Darius had two slices instead of one.

Darius gave Sparky some water and fed him a can of beef stew that had been left out on the counter, which Sparky devoured within seconds. When Sparky was finished eating, Darius took him outside for a short walk and then they went back inside to go to bed. It was late and Darius kept yawning. Even Sparky seemed eager to get comfortable on a large pillow in front of the fireplace. As Darius passed through the living area where Teddy was already sprawled out on the sofa, he said, "Sweet dreams, I'm exhausted and I can't wait to get into bed."

Teddy sent him a smile and said, "Sweet dreams, honey. I sure hope you get some sleep, because those two men don't look as if they're even a little bit tired."

Darius took a quick glance toward the back of the cottage where Strong Man and Butch were already in bed waiting for him. Both were naked on top of the covers and both had erections. They'd just finished kissing each other and it looked as if they'd already begun having fun without Darius. He winked at Teddy and said, "Well, I can't disappoint them. Are you sure you don't mind? I don't want to make you feel awkward. I can tell them to just go to sleep."

Teddy waved his hand. "Oh, I'm fine. I couldn't care less. Just because I don't want to join you doesn't mean I want to ruin your fun. Have a blast, sweetie. I'll see you in the morning."

Darius laughed and turned toward the bedroom area in the back. When he reached the foot of the bed he found Strong Man and Butch flat on their backs with their hairy legs crossed at the ankle, stroking their erections. There was no sense of awkwardness and no sense of shame. Everyone in that house that night, including Teddy on the sofa, understood everyone else and explanations were not necessary. But most of all there was no fear of getting caught and living with guilt. In the Land of Pride lying with another man seemed perfectly normal for men like them and that kind of freedom and abandon was completely new to Darius. So far he'd lived his life sneaking around in barns and in the woods hoping to avoid being discovered. When he realized that his entire existence up until that night in the cottage had been about hiding who he really was, he stood at the foot of the bed and removed his clothes slowly for them. He wanted to do this. He wasn't yawning now. He'd never known what it was like to be normal and he didn't want to waste a moment of that feeling.

When he was naked he climbed onto the bed and crawled up between Strong Man and Butch and gave them both a long kiss on the mouth. Of course he was still wearing the pink glittery stilettos because he couldn't remove them, but Strong Man and Butch didn't seem to care that he was wearing shoes in bed. While they all kissed those two kept running their hands all over Darius' bottom and legs and he finally wound up on his back with both of them practically on top of him.

They spread his legs and lifted his feet higher. As they reached down to play with his bottom, he glanced up and discovered something even more unusual about the cozy little cottage with the adorable little topiaries. Directly above him there was a mirror that mimicked the size of the bed that had been suspended from the tall ceiling. He saw what they were doing to him, he saw himself naked with his legs spread, and he saw both men playing with his hole. Even though he knew deep down he wasn't in love with either of them, he did care about them and his entire body filled with so much emotion his heart began to beat faster. He knew they cared about him as well because they asked him if he was okay and he responded by caressing their backs and saying, "I'm fine. You're both wonderful."

They all kissed for a long time and everything

remained equal. In other words, Darius felt no sense that one of them was more important than the other and there was no competition. Even though Strong Man wasn't very experienced, he watched Butch and followed his every move. They simply moved and acted on instinct and emotion and nothing was forced or rushed this time. As they all kissed, Strong Man and Butch took turns inserting their fingers into Darius' body and stimulated the lips of his anus. He'd always been extremely sensitive there, sometimes more so than with his own erection. Most of his own climax usually came from the nerve endings in and around his anus and that's what created and maintained his erection. And sometimes he didn't even have to have an erection to grow sexually stimulated.

When they stopped kissing, Darius crawled up on his knees and went down on each one of them. He took turns stroking and massaging and sucking their genitals, switching between their dicks and their balls. Darius had always appreciated and loved everything about the male body, however, he loved dick the most. In fact, the only time he ever felt the most at peace with himself, and the most centered, was when he had a man's dick in his mouth and balls up against his chin. There was nothing else like it for Darius. The smell, the texture, and the taste of a man's dick couldn't be compared to anything else in the world. It was so instinctive and it filled him with such a sense of love and satisfaction he grew completely lost in what he was doing and nothing else mattered.

The moment he began to taste their pre-come he started sucking even harder and faster. A man reaching climax in his mouth had always been one of the ultimate sensations for Darius, both emotionally and physically. The taste of a man's come was sweeter than anything and the pleasure it brought to the man he was sucking was intense and genuine. When he realized that he had the ability to give someone else this kind of pleasure he worked even harder to make it better.

On that night it wasn't going to end with two blowjobs. Strong Man and Butch wanted more and they weren't shy about turning him over and climbing on top of his back. Strong Man entered him first and he fucked him for a few minutes in this position, and then he pulled out and Butch took over and they repeated this same pattern in about four other positions for the next hour or so. As each man entered him, he felt a different sensation every time. They weren't shy about manipulating him or moving him around and he allowed them complete control.

He finally wound up on his back in a classic missionary position with both men taking turns and he enjoyed this the most. On his back, in this position, he could glance up at the mirror and watch how they were fucking him and see what they were doing to him and he'd never been able to do that before. At that moment he knew deep down inside he was also creating a memory that would serve him well for years to come. He would always see the image of Strong Man and Butch on top of him, and it would always bring him back to this night in the little cottage. Although none of it made sense, it would be his own private little image and no one could ever take that away from him.

Strong Man came inside him first, and then he pulled out and Butch took over. Butch, of course, was more aggressive and he made the bed rock so fast it moved away from the wall. He moved with such alacrity and pounded so hard the only thing Darius could do was hold on to his shoulders and glance up at the mirror over the bed. There was something pleasant and sweet about it, but there was also something raw and animalistic as well. Butch was one of those men who literally humped and bucked so hard and so fast it looked as if he was trying to breed Darius.

They came simultaneously and Butch rested on top of Darius and remained inside him for a few more minutes. Strong Man had been kneeling on the bed holding Darius' right leg up to make things easier. He lowered Darius' leg gently and got up to use a small bathroom to the right of the bed. While Strong Man was in the bathroom, Butch pulled out and slapped Darius on the bottom. "Thanks for that, pal."

Darius lowered his legs and smiled. "You're welcome." He knew Butch meant well and he didn't take offense. He knew he wasn't in love with either of them and that didn't bother him either. Of course his goal was to find a man and fall in love, but he still wasn't sure that would ever happen. He figured he may as well make the best of what he had going for him and enjoy what little emotional contact he had with men.

And this encounter with all three men was not totally void of emotion or caring. After they all used the bathroom and were finally settled in bed they embraced in a nice, easy comfortable way. Darius remained in the middle, with both men on either side facing him. Strong Man had his arm around Darius' waist and Butch had his around Darius' shoulder. He felt safe in between them, and he slept deeply and well that night. And in the morning, while Teddy was already in the kitchen preparing coffee and French toast for everyone, they took turns fucking him all over again. It was fast because they all wanted to head out early so they could reach the Rainbow City, and Darius was showered and dressed by the time Teddy was pouring coffee. He walked into the kitchen with the pink high heels clicking against the painted wooden floor and said, "Everything smells wonderful, Teddy. I'm so starved I could eat the wall."

Teddy poured him a cup of coffee and sent him a great big smile. "I'll bet you are, honey. After the work out these two gave you I'm surprised you can even walk this morning."

Darius shrugged and smiled. He took a sip of coffee and said, "I feel energized. I've never felt better."

Teddy laughed and turned back toward the kitchen to set the coffee pot down on the stove. "Life is so much easier for sluts."

Darius took another sip of coffee and laughed. He didn't mind and he knew Teddy was only joking. This was another thing about being in Pride that he found interesting. He felt connected to Teddy as well as the other men because they seemed to share the same point of view. It wasn't anything obvious that a stranger could pigeonhole, and yet Darius and Teddy knew and understood each other without having to explain anything. Even though Darius had been having sex with farm hands for a while, and even though he'd known he was sexually attracted to men since his first conscious memory, this was the first time he realized that his connection with other men went deeper than just sex and sexuality. They were more than just men with penises and desires and more than just clichés for the mainstream to laugh at. They thought the same way, they reacted the same way, and sometimes they even had the same campy sense of humor. Even Butch and Strong Man related to Teddy in a comfortable way. In spite of all their differences, they all had this one unspoken factor in common. There didn't even seem to be a word for what they had in common. They were like people who share the same nationality, or share the same religion, but in their case it was even more instinctive because they'd all been born that way.

When Darius realized this, he knew for certain there had to be more to who he was than just sex. There was more to him on a social and on a cultural level than just sex. And that made him sigh and smile with relief and joy. Because when he came to this realization it took away all the shame he'd been taught to feel all his life. He realized that his relationships with other men like himself didn't always have to be sexual.

As they all headed out the door that morning and they reached the silver path, Darius grew even more excited than ever to reach Rainbow City to speak with the Wizard of Pride. Now he wanted to know more about himself, and more about men like him, on a cultural and social level. He was also even more eager than ever to go home to Uranus and he wasn't even totally sure why. He had this feeling there was something special there waiting for him and he wasn't sure what that was, and the Wizard of Pride was the only one who could help him.

Chapter Eleven

They traveled along the sliver path for a few hours and nothing eventful happened. They were passing through a heavily wooded area and Darius was worried. Even though he was still wearing the pink stilettos, he couldn't stop thinking about the Wicked Fairy. He had this feeling she was plotting some kind of revenge to get those shoes back. So when they came to the end of the wooded area and the landscape opened up to a vast open meadow that was filled with pink flowers, he stopped to rest for a moment.

Butch stopped and said, "Would you look at that."

"I've never seen anything more amazing," said the Strong Man.

"It's simply fabulous," Teddy said. "All that pink." He pronounced pink, *pay-ink*.

Even Sparky barked.

Beyond the wooded area with pink flowers, just within their reach, Darius saw nothing but clusters of the most unusual blue flowers with something yellow in the middle. He wanted a closer look, so he stepped up to the edge of where the flowery meadow began and bent down. "I've never seen any flowers like this back in Uranus," he said. "They're like a cross between a blue rose and a peony. And they're so huge. I don't even know what to say about that beautiful yellow thing in the middle of each flower."

Butch stepped up beside him and he glanced down at the flowers. "I know what to say. Looks like a dick to me, honey." He pointed and shook his finger. "That there is a phallus in the middle of that flower."

"Oh Butch," Darius said. Although, he did have to admit the stem in the middle of each flower did resemble a phallus. Each stem had a long, thick shaft and a round bulbous head like a mushroom.

Teddy took a closer look and shook his head. "He's right, hon. These are the *peen* flowers. And there are millions of them. Big blue flowers with stems in the middle that resemble peens of all different sizes. It's like a peen buffet."

Strong Man nodded. "Yup, they look like penis flowers to me."

"Well, I guess they do resemble penises, but they're still beautiful," Darius said. "I just love them."

Teddy laughed. "I'll bet you do, sweetie."

Darius ignored that comment he glanced across the meadow and gaped for a moment. He stood up and pointed to the other side. In the distance, there was the most colorful, unusual city skyline he'd ever seen. From where he stood all the tall buildings had an art deco quality, and the overall look combined all the colors of the rainbow. "That must be it," Darius said. "That must be the Rainbow City. We're almost there, guys."

"Now *that's* impressive," Butch said.

The others nodded in agreement and Darius said, "Let's go. I can't wait to get there."

He ran into the meadow filled with blue penis flowers and the others followed him. Rainbow City didn't seem that far off now and he couldn't wait to get there. For the first time since he'd begun this journey along the silver path, he felt free and safe from the Wicked Fairy, as if nothing could harm him anymore.

When they reached the middle of the meadow with blue penis flowers, Darius felt a little light-headed and he had to slow down. His head felt fuzzy, his eyelids grew heavy, and his legs began to feel as though someone had tied weights to them. Every step forward grew so difficult he finally came to a full stop.

Butch and Strong Man had been a few paces ahead of him. T hey stopped. Butch glanced back and said, "What's wrong? Why are we stopping?"

"I don't know," Darius said. "I just can't seem to take another step forward."

"Me, too," said Teddy. "She can't move her legs."

Then Strong Man yawned and said, "I'm exhausted."

"I feel it now," Butch said. "This is silly but I'd like to lie down right now and take a nap."

After that, they didn't really have much of a choice. The feeling of absolute exhaustion grew so intense there was nothing else for them to do but lie down on a bed of penis flowers. The scent coming from the blue fluffy penis flowers was so intoxicating they didn't put up much of a fight either.

"Let's just rest for a while," Darius said. "We'll be fine after a quick nap. We still have plenty of time to reach Rainbow City before dark."

The last thing Teddy said before he closed his eyes made Darius smile. "Oh, girl, she needs her beauty rest."

The last thing Butch said made Darius wonder. "I think the Wicked Fairy put a spell on this meadow with dick flowers. Dick flowers that make you tired. This is not normal."

Strong Man yawned. "I think you're right. It's the smell of dick flowers all right."

Darius just nodded and closed his eyes. As ridiculous as they sounded, he agreed with them but there wasn't much anyone could do about it now other than hope for the best and sleep. He fell into a deep peaceful sleep and by the time he opened his eyes again he was naked and Strong Man was on top of him, and Strong Man was naked as well. He felt Strong Man's erection pressing into his pelvis and he spread his legs and asked, "What's going on?"

"I'm not sure," Strong Man said. "I don't even remember taking off my overalls. And this erection is unusual. I've never been this hard in my entire life."

Then Darius heard moaning and grunting and he glanced to his right and saw that Butch and Teddy were naked and Butch was fucking Teddy from behind. Butch was saying things like, "Are you my little piggy?" and Teddy was replying with things like, "Oh yes, I'm your little piggy, fuck me," while Butch fucked him. This was so out of character for Teddy that Darius knew this was not normal and something supernatural was happening to all of them.

Strong Man shook his head and pressed his erection into Darius harder. "Would you look at Teddy and the way Butch is fucking him? I've never seen anyone fuck that fast or hard before. I didn't think Teddy liked casual sex. I thought he preferred more emotional sex."

Darius was more erect than usual and he had his suspicions. "This isn't normal. Teddy *doesn't* like casual sex. He would never do anything like this under normal circumstances. I have a feeling the Wicked Fairy put an aphrodisiac spell on all these blue penis flowers and that's why we're all so horny and we all have such extra hard erections. I have to find out if this was consensual for Teddy. I want to know if Teddy consented to this, and if Butch agreed, too."

"But if it's supernatural that won't make sense. It doesn't really matter because supernatural means it's not real."

"This seems different. We both know what's going on and we are both capable of making rational decisions and choices right now, so it's not *that* kind supernatural. Maybe it's just a spell that enhances sexual desires, consensually."

Strong Man looked over at Teddy and Butch and smiled. "I think you're right about one thing. We need to make sure this is consensual."

Butch and Teddy were about 100 feet away. Darius cast a glance in Teddy's direction and asked, "Teddy this is unlike you and I want to make sure you are okay. Are you sure you consented to doing this?"

Teddy was so out of breath he could barely speak. He glanced at them with a great big smile. "Yes, I'm fine. I consented and I wanted to do this. This is consensual sex. You do not have to worry. Nothing untoward is happening here. We are both two grown adults who consented to having sex and we know exactly what we are doing. But thank you for asking. You're a dear friend, Darius. I love you."

"As long as you're okay," Darius said. "That's all

that matters. I wouldn't want to think you were forced into doing something against your will. I'd never let that happen to you."

"I'm good," Teddy said.

Strong Man shrugged. "Well that takes care of that. I guess it was consensual, and this must be a consensual sex spell. What do we do now? I'm so horny right now I could explode."

Darius rested his palms on Strong Man's shoulders and lifted his legs higher. "Fuck me as hard as you can until the spell wears off. It can't last forever and you have my full consent. There's nothing else we can do."

This wasn't just any ordinary consensual aphrodisiac spell either. The moment Strong Man entered Darius' body with his extra hard erection he started fucking him so hard his testicles slammed against the bottom of Darius' ass. With each thrust, Strong Man went deep and Darius experienced more pleasure than he'd ever known. The spell didn't just keep them all hard and horny. It kept them climaxing regularly as well. Darius could still hear Butch and Teddy moaning and now he knew why. While Strong Man fucked Darius they both kept climaxing repeatedly and Darius didn't even have to touch his own penis. This intense fucking became a long stream of constant orgasms that kept repeating every 10 minutes or so and they had no control over their emotions whatsoever. The spell rendered them helpless and they continued to fuck and come until Darius started to wonder if it would ever end.

Then something odd happened. After Strong Man and Darius came once again, a light fleece of snow began to fall from the sky, and then the sky was blue and the sun was still shining. The snow cooled them down and their erections finally subsided. As they grew flaccid and Strong Man slipped out of Darius' body, Darius sighed and said, "I think the spell is wearing off."

Strong Man kissed him on the mouth and said, "I kind of hate to see it end. I lost track of how many times I came inside you."

Darius caressed his neck and said, "I lost track of how many times *you* made *me* come. It was like being in a constant state of orgasm that wouldn't end."

"Well, I for one am flabbergasted," Teddy said. His voice rose up out of the flowers. He was still on his hands and knees, with his back arched and his chubby legs spread, from getting fucked doggie style and Butch was still holding his waist. "I didn't even think I liked sex very much. I've always been more emotional, maybe even asexual. I always preferred cuddling more. But that sure was some good dick. And even though I may never do anything like this again, that was the very best sex I have ever had in my life."

Sparky just lifted his head and yawned. Apparently, he'd slept through the entire event and consensual sex spell hadn't affected him at all.

After they got up, they found their clothes in the flowers, they dressed, and Darius pointed to the other edge of the blue penis flower meadow and said, "There's the silver path again. Let's go. That's going to lead us right into the Rainbow City. I'm so excited."

* * *

At the end of the silver path, they reached the Rainbow City. The city itself was closed off with a rainbow-colored wall so tall and thick that when

Darius glanced up he felt a little light-headed. It was every bit as tall as the skyscrapers Darius had seen in the movies set in New York City and he had no idea how they would get inside. There seemed to be so many obstacles coming in their direction he was starting to wonder if he would ever get back to Uranus.

Butch pointed to a tall set of double doors as high as the wall and said, "I guess that's the entrance."

Darius glanced at the doors and nodded. "And now we have to figure out how to get inside."

Teddy put his hand on his hip and said, "This might sound odd, but we could try knocking. It's been known to work before."

Darius smiled. He loved Teddy's sarcasm and his vicious wit. He sent him a smile. "Let's give it a shot, hon."

Strong Man walked up to the doors first and pounded on them with his fist. After the third knock, a small door just above their heads opened and a crooked little man with thick uneven eyebrows poked his head through an opening and asked, "Who's there?"

Darius looked up at him and said, "We're here." He had puffy silver hair that looked as if he set it in pin curls every night like Darius' Aunt Etienne. In fact, if he'd been wearing lipstick and his eyebrows hadn't been uneven he would have been a dead ringer for Etienne.

The little man blinked. "Well who are you?"

"We're here to see the Wizard of Pride," Darius said.

"Honey, I'm sorry but no one gets to see the Wizard," the man said. "I've never seen the Wizard so what makes you silly people think you're going to see him?"

"The Good Fairy sent me here and she said I could see him," Darius said.

Teddy pointed at the man and started referring to himself in the third person again. "Listen, doll, let's stop playing games here. She's been walking for a long time and her feet are killing her."

"It's true," Strong Man said. "The Good Fairy sent us here and we have proof." He pointed to Darius' feet. "She gave him the pink stilettos. He's wearing them now."

As the man in the door glanced down at Darius' feet, Darius turned his leg a little and moved his foot around so he could see the shoes clearly.

The moment the man saw the shoes his expression grew more animated and he clasped his palms together. "Well now that's a whole different story. My, but they are truly lovely high heels if I do say so myself. And you wear them well, sweetie."

Darius smiled. "Well, thank you very much. Can we come inside now and see the Wizard. It's really very important otherwise I'll never get to see Uranus again."

The man blinked. "My *anus*?"

Butch shook his head. "Not *your* anus. He's talking about his home town called, Uranus."

Teddy snickered. "Honey, nobody wants to see *your* anus."

The man sent Teddy a look. He seemed so excited about the fact that Darius was wearing the pink stilettos he totally ignored Teddy's snarky comment and said, "Well of course you can come inside. I want to get a better look at those shoes."

The man disappeared for a moment, and then a few seconds later the doors leading into Rainbow City opened slowly and Darius reached out to pet Sparky's head. He had no idea what was waiting for them inside this unusual city, or if he would even get a chance to meet this mysterious grand Wizard of Pride. This so-called wizard... or queen... sounded so pretentious and intimidating Darius wondered just how he could command such power over all these people. However, as he glanced into Rainbow City and he saw all the people inside walking around, he knew one thing for certain. He had found a place in the world where he could be with his own kind. They weren't all the same, and he could see the obvious signs of diversity. But they all had one thing in common, which was that they all seemed to fall under one grand, colorful umbrella that made them all different from everyone else in the world. Knowing this gave Darius a sense of calm and a huge sense of pride, which then gave him the strength and power to move forward.

Chapter Twelve

When they crossed through the doorway and entered this place called Rainbow City, Butch glanced around and said, "Well, would you get a load of all this?"

The rest of them stood there gaping in every direction and Darius knew exactly why. It was almost too unbelievable to be true. Behind the tall wide doors stood a magical little city that had been painted in all the colors of the rainbow, along with various other pastel shades of blue, pink, purple and peach. There were too many different colors to name, but that wasn't the most vivid thing Darius saw. The main entry way was filled with people that seemed to come from all walks of life, and stippled in between the people were more of those human-like dogs that Darius had seen earlier when he'd first landed in the Land of Pride. Everyone was dressed differently and colorfully, with no set rule or pattern to follow.

Strong Man pointed at someone and said, "Look, a man wearing a skirt. Would you look at that?"

Teddy put his hand on his hip and smirked. "Well I think that skirt is adorable on him. He has the legs for it."

From what Darius could see without knowing any details, the Rainbow City appeared to be gender neutral and not everyone followed the rules that Darius had always known in society. Of course there were men who dressed in traditional male clothing, and women who wore frilly dresses. However, there were also men in skirts and high heels, and wome n in overalls, plaid shirts and chunky soiled work boots. The only pattern that he could see was that there was no set pattern, and no judgment. It looked as if everyone in the Land of Pride identified in a way that made them feel the most natural and comfortable and no one else critiqued them, and it was the gayest thing he'd ever seen.

Teddy turned and gestured to something and said, "That reminds me of a parade, but not like any parades I've ever seen before."

Darius followed his gaze and smiled. "It does look like a parade, and you're right. It's not like any parade I've ever seen before in Uranus."

There didn't seem to be any automobiles in the Land of Pride. Instead, there were colorful horse-drawn carriages from another century, and these long, flat floats also drawn by horses that reminded Darius of the one Miss Uranus Feed and Grain sat on every year in the annual Uranus Fourth of July parade. These floats were different, though, because they were decorated with all kind of elaborate trimmings. Some had thick fluffy layers of white lace, others had large satin bows, and many had shiny silk buntings draped and swaged in every direction. But more than that, the people riding through the city on these floats all seemed to possess a sense of grandiosity, as if they were proud, elite royalty. And it wasn't because of the way they were dressed, at least not completely. Although some wore fine silk gowns and sheer linen suits, others wore practically nothing. One float that passed by was filled with almost naked men wearing the same kind of leather gear that Butch always wore.

"It's like I died and went to homosexual heaven," said Teddy, with one hand pressed to his chest and the other on his hip. "I've never seen this many good-looking half-naked big furry men in one place in my entire life. It's like a big boy buffet."

Darius smiled. "The women look just as happy, too."

"There don't seem to be any rules here," Butch said.

The instant he said this a long gilded carriage pulled up to where they were standing and the driver tipped his silver hat and said, "That's because there are no rules. You can be whoever you want to be here, without judgment." He spoke with a thick British accent and he was wearing one of those complicated outfits that so many others were wearing, but it was difficult to place a set time period to it. The silk waistcoat appeared French, the wide red hat with a purple plume looked English, and his shirt looked as if it could be made out of Irish lace. From the waist down, he wore a black garter belt, black silk stockings, and black pumps with high heels. Half his outfit had jumped out of an 18th Century French oil painting and the other half had jumped out of a campy burlesque review.

Darius took a step toward the gilded carriage and asked, "Could you please take us to see the Wizard of Pride. We've come an awfully long way and it's really important that we see him."

The driver glanced down at the pink high heels Darius was wearing and smiled. "Of course I can take you there. But first I'll take you to a place where you can freshen up a little. I'm sure you're tired from walking all that way and you'd like to look your best for the Wizard of Pride."

"Oh that would be wonderful," Darius said. "Thank you so much."

After they all climbed into the gilded carriage, the driver took off and Strong Man poked Teddy in the ribs and said, "I've never seen a horse like *this* one."

The horse was pink and white and aubergine, and at the top of its head there was a long pointy cone-shaped horn. Darius had read about them once in a book and he smiled and said, "It's not a horse. It's a unicorn. It's a mythical animal."

"I'm not sure I understand any of this," Butch said, "but I do find it all interesting. There doesn't seem to be any shame or self-loathing here."

On the way to wherever the driver was taking them in Rainbow City, Darius glanced in every direction so he wouldn't miss a single thing. There were shops filled with colorful flowers and the bakeries overflowing with the finest French pastries he'd ever seen. He noticed that a lot of the people walking were wearing outfits that either had rainbows on them, or were actually the colors of the rainbow. This one specific rainbow theme seemed to follow through everywhere he looked. And the names of the side streets were even more interesting. Back home in Uranus all the streets had been named after former Presidents or prominent local people. In the Land of Pride each side street seemed to have a theme. He passed a street called Penny Lane on the left that had a musical appeal, and then he passed another with many trees that had been named Russian River. There was a street called Provincetown Alley that had a nautical look, another called The West Village Lane that appeared more urban, and another had been dubbed Gay Street. Even though all of this was totally foreign to Darius, all these names sounded so familiar to him.

As they continued on toward their destinations, the driver glanced back and said, "After you freshen up we'll go to tea dance and then I'll set up an appointment with the Queen of Pride."

Darius looked up at him. "What's tea dance?"

"Oh, I'm sorry. I forgot. You wouldn't know that yet," said the driver. "Tea dance is a ritual here every single day in the Land of Pride with the men. Of course for the women it's optional, but at 5:00 in the afternoon, the men all get dressed up and meet at the bars for drinks and music and socializing. It's the best part of the day. No one misses it."

"Well that sounds wonderful," Darius said. "I love tea."

Teddy laughed. "I don't think they really drink tea there, hon, not unless it's spiked with a little gin and regret."

They passed a few more side streets with unusual, unfamiliar names, like Harvey Milk Way and Brokeback Alley, and the carriage came to a halt in front of a plain simple building that reminded Darius of his high school gymnasium. A sign above the door read, "The Fraternity Bathhouse," and below that in smaller print it read, "For all your manly needs and desires." Darius had been expecting something more along the lines of a hotel or a hostel, but this place reminded him of the YMCA back in Uranus.

Butch didn't seem upset. He smiled and said, "Oh, this is going to be fun."

"What's a bathhouse?" Darius asked. It sounded like something from Roman times.

Teddy laughed and he poked Strong Man in the ribs. "I'm not sure, but it sounds like something you're going to love, Darius."

They climbed out of the carriage and two tall attractive young men in their 20s wearing football uniforms greeted them at the door of The Fraternity Bathhouse and opened the double doors so they could enter. Oh, Darius had always loved the football players at his school in Uranus but he never dared to even think about them for fear of backlash and shame. As much as he'd always wanted those football players he knew that would never be part of his reality. Those football players who dated cheerleaders would have laughed at men like Darius, or worse. If they'd known that Darius was even slightly interested in them they might have beaten him to a bloody pulp.

But these young college jocks in sports uniforms seemed so friendly and nice. The moment they entered the bathhouse several more beautiful young men in their 20s who wore baseball uniforms greeted them and a tall one with ginger hair said, "We'll take each of you to the appropriate places. Just come with us."

A young man reached out to take Sparky's leash and Darius pulled back. "Oh, you can't take my dog. He's with me."

The young man in the baseball uniform smiled at Darius and said, "Dude, don't worry. He'll be fine. We'll get him bathed and groomed while you're showering with the football jocks. You have nothing to worry about here in the Land of Pride."

Butch patted Darius on the shoulder. "It's okay. He'll be fine."

Then that young jock took Sparky off to be groomed, and another reached out to take Darius somewhere else. They all split up and went with the young jocks in different directions and Darius figured they would all meet up again after they freshened up.

The handsome young jock in the baseball uniform guided Darius by the hand to the back of the building and they reached a set of double doors that said, "Football Player Locker Room." The guy released Darius' hand and said, "Here you go. Just enter through those doors and the guys will take very good care of you."

"Where did my friends go?" Darius asked.

"Oh, they'll be just fine," the guy said. "They took Teddy to a fabric shop because she's more interested in fabrics than men. They took Butch to a sauna filled with sweet little submissive bottoms because he loves to fuck so much. And they took Strong Man to the special glory hole room because he loves to get sucked off. And you're here at the football players' locker room because you love to be with jocks, but strong jocks with hairy legs and fuzzy arm pits."

Darius tilted his head to the side and said, "Well, you seem to know us all very well."

"You have to remember, dude, there are no secrets, no regrets and there is nothing shameful in the Land of Pride," he said, and then he turned and left Darius standing there all alone.

Darius wasn't sure why this young jock was calling him dude, but he had to admit it stirred a few feelings deep in his groin. He wasn't sure what was behind the locker room doors waiting for him but he stepped forward anyway. Normally, he never would have entered a men's locker room wearing pink glittery high heels, short pants, and a black tuxedo jacket. He would have pretended to be masculine just like the football players, and he would have made him think he was one of them. But he kept remembering that nothing was shameful in the Land of Pride and nothing bad could happen to him while he was there.

He pushed the double doors open and stepped into the locker room. He inhaled the sweet damp scent of young men showering and shaving and drying their strong firm bodies with damp towels. He took another deep breath and closed his eyes for a moment and listened to the sound of young men with deep throaty voices horsing around toward the back. They were laughing about something and using the word fuck a lot. They sounded just like the guys on the football team he'd known and he moved forward to see what they were doing.

When he entered the locker room area he found 10 beautiful young men in their 20s standing around lockers with wooden benches in between. Some of the men were still wearing their football uniforms, some had stripped down to their jock straps, and some just had towels wrapped around their naked waists. There were a few blond men, a few with dark hair, and a couple had ginger hair. Their strong young bodies ranged from tall and lanky to short and stocky, and each one had large, strong hands. It was one magnificent buffet of every type of man that Darius had ever been attracted to and he didn't know where to look first. He just stood there gaping at the men until one of them turned and said, "C'mon, man. Get in here and take off your clothes so we can hit the showers."

Darius blinked. "Hit the *showers*?"

A blond guy poked a hairy jock on the ribs with his elbow and laughed. "Yeah, man. We've got to get you in the showers and freshen you up, if you know what I mean." Then a few more laughed and they started punching each other.

The room was filled with so much masculinity and testosterone Darius almost grew light-headed. He crossed to a bench in the middle of the locker room where all 10 men were standing and he slowly removed his tuxedo jacket. Then he removed his bow tie and reached out to squeeze a football player's bicep and said, "I'm afraid I can't remove the shoes, guys. I'm not allowed to do that."

Another jock came up from behind and grabbed him by the waist. "That's fine with us. We don't mind in the least." Then that guy slapped his ass and another grabbed him by the shoulders and kissed him on the mouth.

After that, the guys lifted Darius up and carried him into the showers where he went down on his knees and took turns sucking their dicks. Even though they treated him with respect, and he gave them total consent, they laughed and made crude remarks about how much he liked dick and how good he was at sucking dick. It was as if they knew what he wanted to hear in order to continue and to make this experience even more erotic. The more they commented on what he was doing to them, the harder he worked. He sucked their balls, licked their legs, and even got down on the floor to lick their feet. This group locker room scene had always been one of his all-time sexual fantasies and he was not going to let it go to waste. He knew this would probably never happen again and that he would never be with 10 hot young football players in their 20s in a men's locker room shower.

After he sucked their dicks they lifted him up and turned him over in the showers. A tall dark jock pushed him up against the wet beige tiles and Darius spread his legs willingly. He knew what was next and he wanted it. His heart was racing and he wanted these men to take turns on him. As Darius arched his back, the tall young jock rubbed his dick with something clear and shiny and he entered Darius from behind while the other guys in the shower watched and cheered him on. He slid in easily and fucked Darius for a minute or two, and then he pulled his cock out so another one of the jocks could step up and take his turn on Darius.

For the next hour, Darius took all 10 of them, one by one. They pulled him, twisted him, and took turns fucking him until each one of them came. They came inside him, and when they pulled out they patted his bottom and thanked him. And by the time the last football player stepped up to fuck him, Darius was ready for his own climax. He'd already been edging on orgasm since they'd started to take turns fucking him and now he was ready to come, too.

The last football player who fucked him in the showers that day was the tallest, the strongest, and he had the biggest dick. He entered Darius from behind with such force he lifted him up a few inches from the shower floor and pinned him flat up against the tiles with nothing to support him except for the guy's huge cock. And then he fucked him in this same position until they both came together, while the rest of the football players stood on the sidelines and cheered the biggest guy on. They said things that brought Darius even closer to his climax, things like, "Go deep, buddy. Fuck that tight hole, man. Get in there, pal." They all seemed to take such pleasure in watching this big guy fuck Darius that Darius wound up coming without touching his own dick once. And when it was over the big guy who'd fucked him last gently lowered him to the shower floor and he pulled his dick out slowly. Before he left, he kissed Darius on the mouth and said, "You're adorable, man."

After that, Darius finished showering while the football players rubbed soap all over his entire body. They all took turns cleaning him and drying him off, and then they helped him get dressed again. He'd never had this much attention, especially from all these rugged athletic men, and he thanked him all on his way out the door. They were the nicest group of guys, and he felt no shame whatsoever. He left the men's locker room feeling energized and empowered, and ready to meet the Wizard of Pride.

It would have been the most perfect afternoon of his life if it hadn't been for what he found outside waiting for him. He saw his friends standing a few feet away, and Sparky was wagging his tail. But when he glanced up at the sky his heart began to race with fear and he pressed his palm to his stomach gulped. The Wicked Fairy had been flying around above the Rainbow City. She'd left him a message in dark black smoke that read: "I'm coming for you Darius. You can't hide from me, you little slut."

Chapter Thirteen

Everyone in Rainbow City glanced up at the sky and saw the nasty message the Wicked Fairy had left for Darius and they grew stunned with panic. At first they froze, then they gaped at each other, and then they all started running for the doorway that would lead them to the Wizard of Pride. It was hard for Darius to believe that just a moment earlier he'd felt so light-hearted and gay.

Darius, Sparky, and his friends followed the fluttering people, running the entire way, and everyone stopped outside the Wizard of Pride's tall silvery doors. They were majestic, double doors with a golden crown in the middle of each one. The funny looking man with the eyebrows who'd met Darius and his friends at the entrance earlier was standing in front of the intimidating sliver doors, as if he'd expected them. He seemed to be the one in charge of everything in the Rainbow City. He lifted both arms and said, "Stop. Everything is under control and the Wizard of Pride is handling the situation. You have nothing to worry about, so go back to your business and everything will be fine."

For a few seconds, they all stood there hesitating, and then they all turned slowly to return to whatever they had been doing before the Wicked Fairy left the message for Darius in the sky. It was amazing for Darius to watch their resilience, as if they had total and complete confidence that the Wizard of Pride would take care of them.

Darius and the others continued toward the doors and the man with the eyebrows said, "Stop. Go back to your business." He was glowering in their direction and his thick uneven eyebrows were turned downward.

Darius wouldn't back down. He'd come too far to be turned away. "But we have to see the Wizard. It's very important. Please tell him we're here. At least let him know."

The man growled a few times, and said, "No one sees the Wizard. It's forbidden."

Teddy frowned. "But honey, I just got my hair done." Apparently, while Darius had been in the locker room with the football players Teddy had been in the salon getting a makeover. His hair was puffier and curlier than usual.

Butch stepped forward and stared into the man's eyes. "See here, this is Darius. He's the one the Wicked Fairy wants. We must see the Wizard of Pride. We demand you take us to him."

After he said that, the man blinked a few times and said, "Oh, well that's a different story. You're *that* Darius? The Wicked Fairy's Darius?"

Strong Man nodded and pointed to Darius' feet. "That's exactly who he is."

The man turned and looked down at Darius' feet. "Oh my, I see what you mean. Wait here. I'll see what I can do."

As the man crossed to the large silver doors and went inside to see about the Wizard of Pride, Darius turned to Teddy and said, "Oh, I'll finally get to see Uranus again."

Teddy laughed and said, "And I'll get to be masculine, honey. I'll be all man. I'll be so masculine I'll be toxic."

"I'll find out who I am and I'll stop stammering," said Strong Man.

Butch shrugged. "And maybe I won't hate myself so much anymore."

Darius put his palm on Butch's stomach and said, "I sure hope so, Butch. You're a wonderful man. I certainly don't hate you. I wish you could see how wonderful you are."

Teddy smiled. "You're a real sweetheart deep down, Butch."

"Ditto," said Strong Man.

For a few more minutes, they spoke about seeing the Wizard again, and their voices filled with hope when they mentioned the wonderful, magical things the Wizard could do for them. Darius began to feel hopeful about the future and Sparky started to lick his face. Unfortunately, their animated moods didn't last for long because the man with the eyebrows returned quickly and threw both arms up above his head again. "Go away. The Wizard can't see you today." Then he turned his back on them before they had a chance to question him and he disappeared behind the tall silvery doors.

Strong Man shook his head and glanced down at his shoes. "I knew it was too good to be true. I'll never find out who I am."

Butch shrugged. "I guess I'm destined to hate myself for the rest of my life."

"And I'll never be a real man," said Teddy. "I'll never know how to be masculine."

Darius felt a sting in his eye. He started to think about the fact that he might never get to see Uranus again. "Oh, I'll never see the farm and my aunt and uncle again. Etienne raised me like her own child and I'll never be there for her now, to take care of her in her old age the way she took care of me as a child. She defended me against Agnes McCain and now I'll never see her again."

Darius wiped a few tears from his eyes. Then a voice sounded from behind them. Evidently, the man with the eyebrows who had just told them to leave had been listening to them behind the doors and he was now crying, too. "Stop that. I can't stand to see anyone cry. Stop that this instant. Come on inside and we'll figure something out." Then he opened the silvery doors wider and gestured for them to enter the private area that would lead them to the Wizard of Pride.

They followed him through the vast doorway into a long hallway that had been tiled with all the colors of the rainbow. There were no windows or doors in sight and Teddy stopped and said, "I'm claustrophobic, girls. I can't do this. I'm going back."

"But you'll never get to see the Wizard of Pride," Darius said.

"And you'll never be the man you want to be," Butch said.

"It's okay," Strong Man said. "You can do this. We're here for you."

Teddy glanced around at the closed walls and made a face. "I'd just as soon wait outside. She's just not well for this."

Darius grabbed him by the arm and said, "Now you stop that. You're coming with us and that's that. So buck up and let's move forward."

Teddy swooned a little and said, "Okay, sweetie, but she's not liking this one bit."

"The Wizard will be proud of you," Strong Man said.

Teddy shot him a glance. "Honey, right now I'm a scared silly queen. I just want to get through today. If I can get through today, I'll be okay tomorrow."

"That's the spirit," Darius said. "Let's go."

They walked a little longer, and then they reached another set of tall silvery doors. As they stepped closer, the doors slowly opened and a deep, intimidating voice coming from loud speakers addressed them. "I am the Wizard of Pride. The all-powerful and almighty Queen Wizard of them all. I'm the Wizard of Pride, the Queen Mother, and the Queen of all Queens."

Teddy put his hand on his hip. "Well, get her."

At first they didn't know who was speaking to them. The large room was almost completely empty, except for a long, elaborately carved white marble console table against the back wall. There were tall golden torch lights burning on either side of the marble console and that seemed to be the focal point of the entire room. The deep, loud voice seemed to be echoing from nowhere in particular, but then a fantastical, smoky image suddenly appeared above the white marble console and said, "Who are you people and what do you want?"

Darius and the others exchanged a few glances, then Darius stepped forward and bowed to the smoky, exaggerated image of the Wizard. "My name is Darius and we've come a long way to see you. I would like to see Uranus before it's too late."

The Wizard's eyes bulged. "You wanna see my *what*?"

"*Uranus*."

Butch shook his head. "He's talking about the town where he's from. It's a town called Uranus."

"You're the slut named Darius who just took on all those hot young football players," the Wizard said. "You sure don't know how to say no to men."

"Well I don't like to think of it that way, and there's no need to be rude," Darius said. He wasn't fond of being called a slut, not even by the Wizard of Pride. "I like to think of it as being a good sport. Those guys all thanked me when I left. They were grateful. And yes, I like sex and I like men. There's nothing wrong with that."

Teddy giggled.

Darius sent Teddy a look and said, "Well, maybe I am a slut, and maybe I do enjoy men a little too much sometimes, but at least I'm honest about it and I'm not hurting anyone."

"Silence," said the Wizard. "You talk too much. You never stop talking. If there's one thing I can't stand it's a person who tells a long story. I know why you're all here. I know everything about each one of you." While puffs of rainbow colored smoke rose up into the air surrounding the Wizard's image, he rattled off the reason why each one of them had come to see him. His voice grew deeper and angrier and he insulted them all and referred to them with pejoratives that are rarely heard in public.

By the time he got to Teddy and started belittling

him and calling him all kinds of nasty names, Darius' face was the color of beets. He stepped forward with clenched fists. "How dare you speak to him that way? He's the sweetest man I've ever met and you're nothing but a bully who takes the joy out of everything. You call yourself the Wizard of Pride and yet you don't even know the meaning of the word pride. You should be ashamed of yourself."

"Oh stop complaining, you silly little queen," the Wizard of Pride said. The rainbow colored smoke was still billowing and the torches were still burning. "I'll take care of each of you in my own good time, and I'll grant your requests, but in this world nothing comes for free, not even here in the Rainbow City. You'll have to prove yourselves worthy and the only way for you to do that is to go out there and bring me back the wings of the Wicked Fairy."

Butch made a face and said, "We can't do that without killing her, and that is one mean old fairy."

"He's right," Darius said. "How can we ever go up against the Wicked Fairy? We're nothing special."

"She scares the hell out of me, hon," Teddy said, glancing down at his fingernails. "She's one mean fairy, that's for sure."

"Silence! " said the Wizard as his great colorful flames flickered around his image "I've spoken and this is my demand. You must prove yourselves worthy for me to grant you all your wishes. Now go out and get me those wings and don't come back here until you have them."

Teddy shook his head and put his hands on his hips. He faced the image of the Wizard and spoke with a soft, timid voice. "But Honey, if I could kill a

Wicked Fairy I wouldn't even be here. In case you haven't noticed, I'm not exactly the most masculine guy in the world. And I just got my hair done, too." He patted the back of his head gently and smiled.

The rainbow smoke and the flames on both sides of the Wizard's image grew thicker and taller and the Wizard let out a loud, vicious growl. "Stop wasting my time and go. Go now and get me those wings."

A loud bang, like that of someone slamming a fist on a table, rattled the room. Teddy's eyes grew wide with fear. His entire body began to shudder and he turned and ran for the doors. Darius and the others followed and tried to catch up with him so they could calm him down, but it was no use. The moment he reached the end of the hall where they'd entered, Teddy jumped straight through the first window he saw.

Thankfully, they weren't up that high and they found Teddy outside the Rainbow City tangled in bush that grew cotton candy. They helped him climb down from the bush and brushed pink cotton candy off his clothes.

"We have no choice. We have to do this. We have to figure out how to get the Wicked Fairy's wings. I want to get back to Uranus and the rest of you want your requests granted. There's no other way, " Darius said.

Teddy took a quick breath and put his hands on his hip. He spoke with his thickest southern accent. "I hate to say this, hon. I really do hate to say this, but I think you're right this time. We have to get that mean old fairy's wings." When he said, fairy, Darius smiled because it sounded like *fay-ree*.

Chapter Fourteen

They were told the only way they could reach the Wicked Fairy's castle was through one of the darkest, most dangerous, cruising forests in the land. It was called The Wicked Fairy's Forest. Nothing was safe for people like them in this forest of the darkest kind of hate and homophobia, and people like them were treated like criminals at best. As the man with the eyebrows escorted them to the rear exit of the Rainbow City, Darius began to feel unsafe and unprotected the moment he stepped outside and heard the door slam behind them.

Butch sent Darius a glance and said, "It can't be that bad. We all know what it's like in the real world and we've all been conditioned to remain discreet at all times. We know hate and shame better than anyone. We've lived it all our lives."

"I don't know about that," said Teddy. "This place gives me the creeps." He looked up at a sign that had been posted to a tall dark tree trunk and read it aloud. *"Good Christian Conversion Therapy Institute 10 Miles."* There was an arrow pointing to the left and Teddy shuddered. "That's one of those places where they say, 'pray the gay away .'"

"I've heard of places like that," Strong Man said. "That's where they take men like us and try to turn us into heterosexual men. They call it *The Cure*. They make us sleep with women."

Teddy swooned. "Oh, dear God in heaven I am NOT doing that."

Darius sent him a look and said, "I've never heard of anything like that. Is that even possible? Besides, I never felt as if I needed to be cured."

Butch shook his head. "Of course it's not possible, even I know that. But they think it's possible. The good Christians and the heterosexuals who think we're criminals and who think we're psychologically damaged believe they can 'cure' us. I've seen it before myself."

"Well I don't think we have to go in *that* direction," Darius said. "They told us to just head straight forward on this brown path of weeds until we reach the Wicked Fairy's castle." The uneven, unkempt path was so ugly it hurt his feelings.

"But that doesn't mean there won't be other obstacles along the way," Teddy said. "This could be dangerous. We could be heading into a different kind of hate for men like us, the likes of which we've never known."

"He's right," said Butch. "We should all stick together right now. No one leave the group. I don't trust anything about this forest."

Darius was still confused. "I'm still not even sure what a cruising forest is. It doesn't sound bad."

Strong Man smiled. "You really are a novice. A cruising forest is a place where men like us meet for discreet sex. It's a secret hiding place because we can't be seen in public. It doesn't always have to be a forest. It could be a park, a public rest room, or even a secluded beach. This is the only way most of us can meet in private, because we're not allowed to meet in public like everyone else. We don't have any other choice but the sneak around in the dark."

"What's so dangerous about that?" Darius asked.

"You never know what can happen," Butch said. "Heterosexual men find it amusing to go to places like this and beat us up, the police find it amusing to bait us into thinking they want to have sex with us and then they arrest us, and then there are the criminals who rob us and leave us for dead. We must be on guard at all times. Anything can happen here. You can't trust anything."

Darius nodded and Sparky barked. "Then we'll stick together no matter what."

Teddy nodded. "Let's roll, girls, before I lose my nerve and turn back."

A few miles down the dark, weed covered brown path, they came across another sign. Darius read it aloud. "Wicked Fairy Castle. Proceed with Caution." The arrow on the sign was pointing to the right.

Teddy looked up and down, and then left and right, and said, "Maybe we should turn around now. This is getting creepy. If we start running now we can reach Rainbow City where it's safe."

"No, Teddy," Darius said. "We can't do that. We have to continue. This is too important, and we've come this far."

Before anyone had a chance to say another word, something fell from a tall tree on the other side of the path and Darius glanced down to see what it was. "It looks like a spice bottle, a very small spice bottle with writing on the label."

As Darius bent over to pick up the small bottle,

Butch glanced at a sign on the tree trunk and said, "This is a *Popper* Tree."

"What's a Popper Tree?" Teddy asked. "I've heard of Poplar Trees, but never Popper Trees."

Butch shrugged. "I'm not sure."

"What does it say on the label?" Strong Man asked.

Darius glanced down at the small bottle in his palm and said, "It just says, Locker Room Man Scent, Inhale Slowly."

"Let me see that," Butch said. He took the bottle, removed the cap, and lifted it to his nose. He pressed one nostril shut with his index finger and inhaled through the other nostril. A second later, his eyes opened wide, he smiled, and said, "Well that certainly was refreshing." Then he inhaled again and reached around to pat Teddy on the behind.

"I think it's some sort of aphrodisiac," said Strong Man.

"We shouldn't mess around with it," Darius said. "We can't trust anything here."

Butch nodded. "You're right. I'll just put this away in my pocket and check it out later when it's safe." He didn't seem to want to let go of the small bottle and Darius didn't feel like challenging him.

After that, they moved forward on the path that was supposed to lead them to the Wicked Fairy's castle and they came to a small lean-to shack with a moss covered roof and broken down clapboards. The sign over the door said, "Men's Room. Men Only."

"We may as well stop and use the rest room now," Darius said. "We may not see another one for a while. I hope it's clean."

As he took a step forward, a stranger exited the

Men's Room and leaned against a crooked wooden post next to the entrance. It was a tall young man, with long black hair, and he wasn't wearing a shirt. His pants were so tight his crotch bulged and his zipper was halfway down. He was wearing cowboy boots and a great big smile. He nodded at Darius and reached down to grab his crotch in the most obvious way, as if trying to lure him into the men's room for sex.

Darius took one look at this young man and his heart began to race. He was so attractive it made Darius smile and he grew instantly erect just looking at him. "Oh, guys. I definitely have to use that rest room now. You just wait here, this won't take long." He figured he would go inside, pull down his pants, and let this guy fuck him fast.

Teddy laughed. "There she goes again. She's in slut mode. She just can't resist a man."

Butch grabbed Darius by the shoulder and said, "No. It's a trap. He doesn't want to have sex with you. He's just teasing you into making the first move. He's trying to lure you into his trap. This is what they do. I've seen it before many times and it even happened to me once in a men's room at a public park. They bait men like us with good-looking cops and then they arrest us and put us in jail. And we have no choice but to plead guilty. It's a practice of shame and humiliation that's been going on for years."

Darius wasn't so sure he agreed. "But a cop would never grab his crotch in such an obvious way. I think this guy looks legitimate. He looks kind of sweet." He couldn't take his eyes off this guy's bulging chest muscles.

Strong Man and Teddy shook their heads at the

same time. Strong Man said, "I agree with Butch. This guy is too good to be true. It's trap all right. I think we should get out of here as fast as possible before we all wind up in jail."

Darius didn't have time to protest. They grabbed him by the arms and whisked him away from the men's room without glancing back once. They all ran most of the way and didn't slow down until the men's room was well out of sight. By that time they were all out of breath. they decided to stop near a large rock to rest for a moment.

"This has to be the creepiest place I've ever been," Darius said, as he rested his palm on Sparky's back. "I can't wait to get back to Uranus now."

Butch sat down on the rock beside him and said, "It is pretty bad, and I've seen a lot of dark places in my life."

Strong Man shrugged. "At least we have each other, there's that. It's better than being alone in a place like this."

Teddy smiled and rested his palm on Darius' shoulder. "That's right, sweetie. It could be worse. We could be all alone here in the middle of this dark fairy forest."

Darius heard a noise from above and he had a feeling they'd spoken too soon. It sounded as if a loud swarm of bees was heading in their direction. He stood up and looked at the sky. In the distance, high above the tall dark trees, he saw a massive swarm of specks flying in their direction. At first he couldn't tell what they were, but as they grew closer he saw that they were men, all good looking, well-built men wearing nothing but red loin clothes. They were almost naked and barefoot, and they all had these large sets of red feathery wings attached to their backs. But more than that, they were all identical in appearance, as if they'd all been cloned, with blue eyes, blond hair, strong muscular bodies, and tight round asses. He pointed upward and shouted. "What in the world is that?"

Butch and Strong Man looked up, and Butch said, "They must be the Wicked Fairy's army."

"Oh dear," said Teddy. "We're being invaded by the *Fairy* Army."

"We have to run," Strong Man said. "We have to get out of here now."

Butch grabbed Darius by the arm and they all ran forward toward the Wicked Fairy's castle. At least they tried to run forward. They didn't get very far. The Fairy Army of beautiful young, identical and almost naked men swooped down from the sky and swarmed around them making it impossible to move. They scared Teddy so much he ran behind a tree and covered his head with his arms. They knocked Butch and Strong Man down on the ground and one of them picked Darius up and lifted him into the sky. Then another one grabbed Sparky, while Teddy, Butch and Strong Man watched from the ground, and Darius screamed, "Help me. Please help me," all while hopelessly flailing his arms and kicking his feet.

The fairy warriors were too powerful and fast for Darius' friends. There was nothing anyone could do. he was now on his own. He had no idea where they were taking him or what would happen to him, but he knew he was safe as long as he was wearing the pink glittery stilettos.

They flew him in the direction of the Wicked

Fairy's castle, which was set high atop a crooked mountain surrounded by thick black clouds against a gray sky. The castle itself was made out of the blackest stone Darius had ever seen. Just like the mountain, the castle was also crooked and bent out of proportion.

There was only one large open window in the entire castle and that's where they took him. They flew right into the open window and set him down on a stone floor directly in front of the Wicked Fairy. A second later, another fairy warrior flew through the window with Sparky and set him down beside Darius. The moment the fairy warrior released Sparky, Darius threw his arms around Sparky's neck and said, "I'm so glad you're safe."

Sparky barked and licked his face.

Then Darius looked up and glanced around the room. There was a massive walk-in fireplace, a long, tall wall of stone, and one of the most exquisite pumpkin pine p lank floors he'd ever seen. Darius had always had a good eye for fine rooms with simple, classic design elements, and this room had it all. Unfortunately, it also had these odd looking pieces of furniture he'd never seen before. With just at a quick glance he knew they were awful. The furniture had a dream-like futuristic appeal. Large over-sized fake leather couches that reclined along with built-in cup holders. Low coffee tables made out of vinyl with fake glass, and side tables to match. The art that on the walls consisted of cliché landscapes, and a few that looked as though they had been painted on velvet. Even though it was all so foreign to him, he knew deep down that this had to be one of the most poorly decorated rooms he would ever see.

The Wicked Fairy took a few steps towards him

and scowled. Darius stood up fast and said, "Let me go. I want nothing from you." But that was a lie. He looked at the wings on her back. He needed them to get back home; back home to Uranus. He wondered if he could just snatch them.

"I'm the one who makes the rules around here, my little slut," said the Fairy. "I tell you what to do, not the other way around."

"What do you want from me?"

The Wicked Fairy glanced down at Darius' feet and pointed with a crooked finger. "I want those high heels. They belong to me now."

"Then take them," Darius said. "I never wanted them in the first place. Take them and let us go."

The Wicked Fairy lifted both arms, and with one swift dramatic gesture she pointed to the pink high heels. Nothing happened. She tried snapping his fingers and nothing happened. "They're stuck," she said. "Give them to me."

"If I could give them to you I would, but I can't get them off either."

"You're lying," the Wicked Fairy squealed. She snapped her fingers. Two of the naked fairy warriors appeared in the open window. "Take him to the tower and lock him up. I'll figure out what I'm going to do with him later. And take the dog, too. Maybe if he has some time to reflect he'll give me back those shoes. And if he doesn't I'll drown that dog next."

The almost naked identical fairy warriors grabbed Darius and yanked him out of the room. Sparky barked and he followed them down a long winding hallway to a set of narrow stone stairs. They hooked a leather collar and a dog leash up to Darius' neck, pulled him up four flights of stairs, and, once at the top, they shoved him and Sparky into a tower room where two more identical fairy warriors were there waiting for him. The two that had pulled him up there were about to slam the door shut when Sparky took off alone and dashed back down the steps. Darius told Sparky to continue running to safety. The two fairy warriors darted after Sparky, but not before slamming the tower door shut and locking it. The best Darius could do now was hope that Sparky would find safety. At least he was free.

Darius turned and glanced at the two almost naked fairy warriors standing on either side of the bed. They had glum expressions and their arms were folded across their chests. Darius was all alone now. The room was dark but at least he could still see enough thanks to a couple of uncovered tiny square windows. There was nothing in the room but a large bed with black sheets and a black headboard. Darius was beginning to wonder about these so-called magic high heels. So far they hadn't done anything but get him into trouble, and he had a feeling there was even more trouble to come.

Chapter Fifteen

For the first time since the Good Fairy had placed the pink high heels on Darius' feet, he felt awkward and slightly ridiculous. It's the first time he'd felt this way since he'd arrived in the Land of Pride and Rainbow City. The context was completely different here in the Wicked Fairy's castle. T here was shame, and guilt, and all the old feelings he'd kept hidden his entire life bubbled to the surface. Now he was alone in a poorly lit room with these two strong, handsome identical fairy warriors and he didn't know what to say or do. He didn't even know if they could speak or think on the most basic level, but he had this feeling after living with years of guilt for being attracted to men that the warriors were judging him for wearing pink stilettos. And the worst part about it all was that he found himself strangely attracted to them in the most profound, unexplainable way.

He took a quick breath and slowly walked over to the warrior on the left side of the bed, with his high heels clicking against the old wooden floor, and he looked him in the eye. He figured he might as well try something. He didn't have much else to lose. "Could you please help me? The Wicked Fairy is going to kill me to get these shoes and I don't even want them. Won't you please try to help me get out of here?"

After he spoke, the one warrior on the left exchanged a glance with the other one on the right side of the bed, and then he glanced at Darius and shook his head. "We follow orders," he said, and then he folded his arms across his chest and looked up at the black ceiling with a blank, robotic expression.

Darius felt his heart beating faster. He looked the fairy warrior up and down and bit his bottom lip. He had long, lean and defined muscles in his arms, his legs, and his abdomen. He had hair on his chest, his legs, and even on his forearms. His beard was thick and his eyes dark brown. His musky masculine scent made Darius unsteady. And the other one was identical to him, which made Darius even more excited. He assumed they were some type of supernatural beings, but that didn't bother him. They still looked human, even up close.

Darius reached out and caressed the warrior's bicep gently. He rubbed the bulging muscle a few times and said, "But no one will know you helped me escape. I'll never tell anyone. And I'd never harm you. You can just say that I tricked you and that it was all my fault. Oh please won't you help me."

Then Darius ran his palm slowly up the warrior's arm and rested it on his shoulder. He was so attractive Darius couldn't resist. Darius didn't want to be rude and he didn't want to assume anything. But he did notice that the warrior's thick flaccid penis had begun to grow erect the instant he touched his arm. If the warrior hadn't been attracted to Darius he would have shoved him away and ignored him completely.

The warrior on the other side of the bed said, "You shouldn't let him touch you that way. He's too hard to resist."

The warrior on the left said, "I can't help it. I like it."

Darius smiled at the warrior on the other side of the bed and said, "I can touch you that way, too, if you like. I don't mind. I can touch you both that way. And you don't even have to do a thing for me. I mean that. No reciprocation." Darius had already reached the point where he couldn't control his urges and he wanted to sample both of these beautiful men. He felt this sudden overwhelming urge to spread his legs and let these men take him. He also figured that if the Wicked Fairy was going to kill him anyway to get the shoes he might as well enjoy one more fling with a couple of extremely good looking men.

The warrior on the left who was already fully erect reached around and rested his palm on Darius' buttocks. He squeezed Darius gently and said, "We don't have to do anything to help you?"

Darius reached down and wrapped his fingers around the warrior's erection and said, "I don't expect a thing from you. If you want to help me, that's fine. But you don't have to help me." Then Darius released his dick and he turned toward the bed.

While both men watched, Darius slowly removed the black tuxedo jacket, the white shirt, the bow tie, and the black shorts. He left the collar and leash on because it made his own erection harder, and he crossed to the other side of the bed naked where the other Warrior was now fully erect. He reached up and put his arms around the warrior's shoulders and planted a wet kiss on the warrior's mouth. Instead of pulling back or pushing Darius away, the other warrior returned the kiss and even pulled Darius up against his naked body.

They kissed for a few minutes while the warrior on the left side grabbed his erection and watched, and then Darius stepped back and turned toward the bed. It was nothing more than a simple queen size bed with a black coverlet and black pillows. He slowly climbed up on the bed, crawled to the middle on his hands and knees, and spread his legs, hoping they would understand his signal and take control.

When Darius arched his back and the warrior on the right grabbed his hips, Darius opened his mouth and started sucking the warrior on the left's dick. The warrior on the right spit on Darius' anus and then he entered him from behind. Darius continued to suck the other warrior's dick while the other slid into him slowly. And when he was deep inside Darius, as deeply as he could go with his pelvis pressed up against Darius' buttocks, he started to rock his hips in a smooth rhythm, fucking him slowly.

It was clear from the start these men were not interested in emotion or foreplay with Darius. It was just like sex with the farm hands back home. As far as Darius knew, they might not have been capable of that. Whether they were human or not, they clearly had urges of their own and the goal seemed to be get in, move fast, and get off. Darius didn't mind: he had a dick in both ends of his body and he enjoyed what they were doing to him. He arched his back and spread his legs wider, encouraging them even further. At one point the warrior on the left pulled his dick out of Darius' mouth and crossed to the other side of the bed so he could take his turn fucking him. He was so eager to mount Darius he shoved the other warrior away so hard he almost knocked him to the floor.

They took turns on Darius in doggy style for a while, and then one of them… Darius couldn't be certain which one because they were identical… grabbed the leash and yanked it hard making Darius gag. One grabbed Darius' ankles and the other took his shoulders and they turned him around in the middle of the bed so they could climb on top of him and take turns this way. Darius was so close to climax by then he just lifted his legs and spread them, and they fucked him in this position until the first one grunted and came inside him. The second one was more aggressive. H e climbed on top and practically folded Darius in half when he came. And when Darius came, he felt the orgasm from the top of his head all the way down to the tips of the pink stilettos that were resting over the fairy warrior's shoulders.

For a moment, they all lay on the bed, breathless and sweaty, with one warrior resting on top of Darius while the pink stilettos dangled over the guy's shoulders. Darius caressed his back and said, "That was very nice. You're both very strong." He meant this, too. By that time he didn't expect anything from these guys. He'd enjoyed them that afternoon and he figured that was as far as it would go. Darius had already resigned himself to the fact that he might never see Etienne again. The Wicked Fairy was simply too powerful for him.

The warrior who was still inside Darius pulled out and flopped to the side of Darius, taking deep breaths as if that was the most fun they'd have in their entire lives. Then both warriors reached down to help Darius climb out of bed. When he was standing, one Warrior said, "Put on your clothes. We don't have much time."

The other warrior nodded. "If you want us to help you, hurry. The Wicked Fairy will be here soon."

"Does this mean you'll help me?" Darius asked.

They both nodded, and one said, "You don't have much time."

Darius threw his arms around one, and then around the other, and he kissed them both and said, "Thank you so much. You'll never know how grateful I am. What will happen to you when the Wicked Fairy finds out? I don't want you getting into trouble."

"Ah well, don't worry about it," said one warrior.

The other one smiled. "We can't stand the Wicked Fairy either. We'll tell her it was the magic shoes."

Darius wasted no time getting dressed. When he was ready, they opened the door and he crept out on his own. He wasn't even sure where he was going, but he ran down the stone stairs as fast as he could in the pink stilettos, so fast in fact that he was a bit impressed with himself. He had to find Butch, Strong Man and Teddy, and then he had to find Sparky and get back to the Rainbow City. He was hoping they were still alive and well and that the Wicked Fairy hadn't done anything to harm them. Darius knew he might never get back to Uranus now, but at least they could live and be happy in Rainbow City with all the other people who were just like they were, without guilt, shame, or judgment. That was better than nothing at all.

As he rounded a corner at the bottom of the stairs, he heard a noise. H e turned to see Sparky sitting on the floor and wagging his little tail, waiting for him. Sparky started to bark and turn around in circles. This was Sparky's way of telling him to follow, Darius knew.

He went down on his knees and hugged Sparky. "I'm so glad you're safe, " said Darius.

Sparky barked again and Darius knew what he was trying to tell him. "You know where Strong Man, Butch and Teddy are, don't you? Take me to them. I'll follow you."

Sparky barked again and ran toward a long dark hallway. He sent backward glances to Darius the entire way to make sure he was following him. They ran as fast as they could, for they knew the Wicked Fairy would be looking for them sooner rather than later. When they reached the end of the long hallway where there was a black door, Sparky barked again and Darius knocked and said, "Are you in there? Can you hear me Butch... anyone?"

The first voice he heard was Teddy's. "Oh, lordy, you found us. Praise be."

Darius tried the door but it was locked. "Yes. I'm here. But I don't know how to get the door open. It's locked tightly and it won't budge."

"Try the magic shoes," Strong Man said. "Maybe they'll work."

"I'm not so sure about that," Darius said. "These magic stilettos only seem to be good at getting men into bed."

Teddy gasped and said, "Did you sleep with those two warriors? I *knew* it. I was taking bets with Butch. I *knew* you'd wind up in bed with them. Damn you're good!"

"Well... they were nice guys," Darius said, with a slight shrug of his shoulders "And they helped me escape, but I would have slept with them anyway."

"Can we discuss this later," Strong Man said. "I'd like to get out of here. Try the magic shoes."

"I'll do my best," Darius said.

He took a step forward. H e glanced down at the pink stilettos, closed his eyes and tightened his fists. He imagined himself turning the knob and opening the door and seeing Teddy, Butch and Strong Man all waiting for him, happy as can be. And when he was ready, he reached for the doorknob. H is fingers touched the metal, then he opened his eyes and saw a spark and a puff of pink smoke. The door that had been locked so tightly opened by itself and they all ran out of the room into the hall where Darius was standing.

Strong Man hugged him and said, "They worked. The magic shoes worked."

Darius glanced down. "I'm stunned."

Butch patted him on the bottom and smiled. "I guess they are good for something besides getting you fucked. I'm surprised you didn't figure it out sooner."

Teddy laughed. He put his hands on his hips and said, "I'm surprised he can even walk after sleeping with those big old hairy fairy warriors. *Lord* have mercy."

Darius knew Teddy was only joking around so he took no offense. Teddy was the kind of man who lived for high camp and he couldn't help himself. His kind of acid wit seemed so basic to his nature that Darius found him more amusing than insulting. Darius hugged him and said, "If it makes you feel any better, they were huge, and I *am* walking with a slight limp."

"I want details, honey," Teddy said.

Butch frowned. "We don't have time for that. Let's get out of here before the Wicked Fairy realizes we're free."

Darius knew he was right and he didn't bother to reply. They all turned back and started running to the other end of the hall, hoping to find a staircase that would lead them out of the Wicked Fairy's castle. At the end of the hall, they ran down four flights of stairs until they reached the main floor. When they reached the bottom of the stairs and glanced over to the right, Darius saw a set of wide double doors that had been left open where he could see the Rainbow City in the distance.

"C'mon," he said. "Let's go. We're almost out of here."

They all turned and started running toward the doors, but just as they reached the threshold the tall double doors slammed shut and a wrecked voice sounded from above. "Oh, not so fast, Darius. You're not getting out of here alive. I want my shoes, you little slut."

They stopped, and Darius felt a sharp pain in his gut. He had a feeling this was it and he would never see Etienne again. He would never see his farm and he'd never see Uranus. But even worse than that, he had this feeling he would be missing something wonderful and important about his life, something significant to his very being, and he wasn't even sure what that was.

Chapter Sixteen

They all leaned back against the locked doors and remained still. Darius glanced up and saw the Wicked Fairy standing on a second floor landing glaring down at them with pinched lips and turned down eyebrows that reminded him of arrows. "I've got you now, all of you, and you're not going anywhere," the Wicked Fairy said. "If you thought you could outsmart me, you were sadly mistaken."

"We're screwed," Strong Man said.

Sparky barked.

"Oh, this isn't good, not good at all," said Teddy.

Darius heard the sound of pounding feet and he glanced to the right and saw hundreds of identical naked fairy warriors rush into the main hallway. They stopped in the middle of the hallway and glared at Darius, Strong Man, Teddy and Butch while the Wicked Fairy laughed and said, "Don't hurt them yet. I want them all captured alive. I'll figure out what to do with them all in good time. I've been in the mood for a boiled dinner."

Teddy clutched his shirt and swooned.

In a dramatic move, the Wicked Fairy lifted both arms and waved them above her head. She repeated some kind of incoherent incantation and then she

147

pitched some kind of fireball with purple smoke down to the first floor where it landed smack in the middle of the naked fairy warriors.

While the naked fairy warriors took a few steps back, Darius closed his eyes and lifted his arms in the air. He wasn't totally sure what he was doing. He wasn't even certain he could do anything. He just kept thinking about the magic stilettos and how they might help him get out of this situation with the Wicked Fairy. If these high heels were magical, he needed them now more than ever. His only thought was to stop the wicked warriors from capturing them and he didn't care how he did it.

He thought long and hard, with his arms and hands stretched forward above his head. He concentrated in breaking free; he focused on running out of there to safety, and all the way back to Rainbow City. And before he even realized what was happening, sharp bolts of white light shot out from his fingertips and up toward the ceiling. When the bolts of sharp light hit the chain that supported a huge black crystal chandelier, it burned the metal chain links and the massive chandelier came crashing to the floor right on top of the fairy warriors.

As Darius, Strong Man, Butch, Teddy and Sparky ran back into the castle hoping to find a safe space, the Wicked Fairy ran down the steps with her arms high in the air and her wings flapping. "Stop them," she said. "Stop them from getting away."

When they rounded a corner, Darius said, "Let's go back upstairs."

"We don't have a choice," said Teddy. "Oh, we're going to die. I just know it."

Darius patted him on the back and said, "But not without a fight."

As they ran toward the stairs and began to climb up to the next floor, the Wicked Fairy and her naked male warriors rounded the same corner. The Wicked Fairy pointed to the stairs and said, "Half of you go up the stairs and the other half go that way. They're not getting out of this castle alive."

Darius and the others kept climbing each staircase, but it was futile; none of them lead anywhere. They didn't know where they were going, but they didn't seem to be heading toward an exit. If anything, they were only burying themselves deeper and deeper into the wicked castle, making it easier and easier for the Wicked Fairy to capture them and turn them into a boiled dinner. The higher they climbed the more dismal the outcome looked, but Darius said nothing to anyone. There was nowhere else to go.

When they finally reached the top of the last staircase they crossed through a door that led them out onto the roof. Butch said, "Go that way," and they followed him toward the roof of a tower.

By the time they reached the tower roof, they saw a band of wicked fairy warriors charging toward them, so they turned and ran back in the opposite direction. A few moments later and another band of warriors charged toward them in the other direction. in a matter of no time they were cornered with nowhere else to run.

They stopped in the center of the roof, trapped and helpless and doomed. The Wicked Fairy appeared at the top of the stairs. She pointed at them and said, "You can't escape from me. This is the end of your journey. You're all going to die slow, painful deaths. The dog will go first into the pot and you will all watch him die. And then I'll cook the rest of you alive, one by one, until the only one left is the little slut who's wearing my magical pink high heels."

As the Wicked Fairy lifted her arms above her head and laughed, Butch pulled a bottle of poppers out of his pocket and removed the lid.

"What on earth are you doing?" Darius asked, gaping at the bottle of poppers in his hand.

Butch shrugged and said, "It takes the edge off. If I'm going to die I might as well die with a good, glorious rush. This thing is good."

As Butch lifted the poppers to his nose to inhale the strong, masculine scent of locker room, the Wicked Fairy reached out to grab Sparky, thinking they were all distracted. But Darius was quick. He lunged forward to stop her. "You're not getting my dog without a fight, you nasty old hag." However, as Darius lunged toward the Wicked Fairy he knocked the bottle of Man Scented Locker room poppers right out of Butch's hand, it sailed through the air, and landed on the Wicked Fairy's head upside down. The clear liquid contents inside the tiny bottle spilled out all over the Wicked Fairy's head and down her crooked vile face. And as the clear liquid alkyl nitrates made direct contact with the Wicked Fairy's skin, she began to moan aloud.

She moaned with such intensity and drama, everyone took a step back, including the naked warriors. She started screaming, "Look what you've done, you little slut." She screamed and pointed at Darius. "I'm vanishing, I'm vanishing. Everyone knows I'm allergic to poppers and I'm disappearing into smoke and ashes. You evil little slut, you and your poppers murdered me."

As the Wicked Fairy continued to disappear into small puffs of smoke, her tacky clothes vanished and her voice trailed off to a faint whisper. Darius couldn't believe what he was seeing. In less than a second or two the only thing left of the Wicked Fairy was the set of wings she'd had on her back.

Sparky ran over to sniff the ground where the Wicked Fairy had been standing only moments ago.

One of the wicked fairy warriors glared at Darius and said, "You've killed her. You've killed her with a bottle of poppers." He seemed to have a speech impediment of some kind and Darius had trouble understanding him.

"Well I didn't know the Wicked Fairy was allergic to poppers," Darius said with a shrug. "No one told me. I didn't even know what poppers were until just recently."

The fairy warrior sent Darius a look and said, "Not all fairies are allergic to poppers. Most fairies love poppers. We can't get enough of them. It's only the mean, sexless, wicked fairies that are allergic to poppers. And you've killed her. You've killed that mean, sexless creature." Then he lifted his arms high above his head while the other naked fairy warriors cheered and said, "Long live Darius. He's killed the Wicked Fairy."

While the fairy warriors cheered, Darius exchanged a glance with his new friends and said, "Can I please have the Wicked Fairy's wings? It's very important."

The fairy warrior who seemed to be the leader bent over, picked up the wings, and handed them to Darius. "They're all yours."

* * *

They returned to the Rainbow City, with Butch carrying the Wicked Fairy's wings. Then the grouchy man with the eyebrows escorted them into the Wizard of Pride's private room and announced their names. They had no trouble getting in this time. All they had to do was show the Wicked Fairy's wings and no one asked any questions.

While they waited for the Wizard of Pride to appear before them, Darius sent Teddy a look and said, "I still can't believe we got those wings. I never thought it would happen."

Teddy put his hands on his hips and laughed. "Honey, never underestimate guys like us. We know what we're doing."

Darius nodded. He had to agree. "I'll say."

Before anyone else could utter a word, a deep voice said, "Why are you back here?" Then an image appeared in a cloudy, hazy form. Once again, the image appeared larger than life, as if it wasn't real at all. It was dramatic, with fire and smoke and greenish blue highlights. Darius realized it was impossible to actually get a clear concise image of the Wizard of Pride.

"I beg your pardon, sir," Darius said. "He stepped forward and faced the peculiar image, then he turned and took the fairy wings from Butch's hands. "We have the fairy wings. We took them right from the Wicked Fairy. She's gone for good now."

As he set the fairy wings down so the Wizard of Pride could see them, the Wizard said, "And just how in the world did you four do that?"

"Well, it wasn't easy," said Strong Man.

"She put up a good fight," said Butch.

"We threw poppers at the old bat and she melted," Teddy said. "You should have seen it."

"Poppers?" the Wizard said.

Darius nodded. "Apparently, some fairies are allergic to poppers."

The Wizard of Pride laughed and said, "So you beat that talentless wicked old fairy at her own game. Very clever, if not amusing."

"Now that we brought you the Wicked Fairy's wings, you can grant our requests," Darius said.

After a moment of silence, the Wizard of Pride said, "Go away and come back next week. I must think about this."

Darius felt his heart sink in his chest. After all that hard work, not to mention all the danger that had been involved, the Wizard of Pride was brushing them off. But Darius wasn't going to stand there and just take it, not this time. He'd been through too much and he wanted to get home, now. "Oh no you don't." Darius marched forward, wiggling a finger at the wizard and his flames. Were the pink stilettos giving him this courage or was it Darius himself? Whichever it was, it felt good. "You promised us that you'd grant our wishes if we brought you the Wicked Fairy's wings and we delivered. Now it's your turn to help us."

Teddy pointed at the fuzzy image and shook his finger, side by side with Darius "That's right, hon. I was standing right here. You promised. I heard it with my own ears."

As they argued with the Wizard of Pride, Sparky walked to the other end of the room not far from the over-sized fuzzy image and stopped in front of a long wall of red silk draperies. He looked up and down a few times, then he lowered his head and took a chunk of red silk fabric in his mouth. With a quick turn of his head and a step back, the red silk drapery slowly opened and exposed the back of a tall man with dark hair. The man was standing in front of some kind of large complicated machinery, and he was pulling levers and pushing buttons. And when he spoke it soon became apparent that this man was really the Wizard of Pride speaking into a microphone, and he'd been there all along creating the illusion that the Wizard of Pride was a fuzzy, mystical image surrounded by smoke and fire.

At first, Darius wasn't sure what to make out of all this, so he walked over to the wall where the tall man with dark hair was pulling levers and said, "What are you doing? Where's the Wizard of Pride?"

While the others walked up behind Darius, the tall man with dark hair tried to pull the red drapery shut and he made a few excuses. He fumbled and stammered to find the right words to reply to Darius. He finally gave up, took a deep breath, and exhaled. "Oh it's no use. I'm the Wizard of Pride."

"That's ridiculous," Darius said. He had to admit that this man was much more attractive than he'd imagined the Wizard of Pride would be. He was wearing a tight black shirt that hugged his chest muscles, tight black pants that made his crotch bulge, and he had large alluring blue eyes. He could have been a movie star.

The handsome man shrugged and said, "I'm afraid it's true."

"That's ridiculous," said Butch.

"You're nothing but a fake," said Strong Man.

Darius looked the Wizard up and down and thought for a moment. "You do seem awfully familiar. Have we met before? Maybe on the side of the road somewhere?"

Teddy rolled his eyes. "Oh no, he slept with this guy, too. He slept with the Wizard of Pride and doesn't even remember. Girl, she's unreal."

The Wizard of Pride looked at Darius and blinked.

"Now wait a minute," Darius said. He looked at Teddy. "I didn't say I had sex with him. I just said he looks familiar, is all. He reminds me of someone but I just can't place him. It's someone I liked very much, someone who made me feel safe and secure for the first time in my life... someone I miss very much."

"Well I think he's a fake and a horrible person," Butch said.

The others began to nod their heads and the Wizard of Pride lowered his voice and said, "I'm afraid I am a fake, but I try to be a good fake if that makes you feel any better. I've never harmed anyone in my life."

Strong Man squared his back and said, "What about your promise? I'll never find out who I am now. I'll spend the rest of my life stammering and worrying."

"Well now, let me see," the Wizard of Pride said. "That's not difficult at all. You already know who you are. You've always known who you are. You, my friend, are a good, decent, sweet man. You just need to make it official." He pulled a rolled up piece of paper out of his pocket and unrolled it in front of them all and said, "This is a birth certificate, signed and dated today. You are now officially Strong Man, the strongest man on earth. And there's nothing odd or unusual about you. You are now perfect and you have the certificate to prove it."

Strong Man took the certificate and lifted his chin higher. When he spoke, this time he didn't stammer. "I know who I am. I finally know who I am. I'm a proud man who loves other men and there's nothing wrong with me. I'm going to be okay."

"What about me?" Butch asked. "I came here to find out why I'm always so aggressive and mean. I'd like to stop hating myself. I guess I want to be honorable."

The Wizard of Pride sent him a glance and said, "I think I have just the right thing for you." He pulled some kind of necklace with a silver medallion out of his pocket and lowered it over Butch's head. "This is the Medal of Honor, and only a few people receive it. You're one of a very lucky few to receive it. You are now officially a man of honor, without shame and without fear. There's no reason for you to hate yourself any longer. And you have to remember this: no one can ever shame you unless you allow them to shame you, and no one can take away your honor unless you allow them to do that. You are, in deed and action, a man of honor."

Butch glanced down at the medal resting on his chest. "I am?"

The Wizard nodded. "Of course you are. You always have been. You no longer have to prove yourself to anyone. You are now officially a man of honor and you never have to pretend to be anything else."

Butch stepped back and smiled. He rested his fingertips on the medal and said, "I feel so much better now. I don't feel angry and I don't feel the need to be too aggressive. I actually like who I am and I don't have to prove anything to anyone anymore."

As the Wizard turned, Teddy put his hands on his hips and spoke with his thickest southern accent and his highest effeminate voice. "What about me, hon? What about what I need? I'm tired of people laughing at me and calling me names like sissy. I want to be a real man just like Darius, Strong Man and Butch. I don't want to lisp or have a limp wrist. I just want to be normal. I want to be a manly man, big and strong and manly." When he said the word manly he curtsied and batted his eyelashes.

The Wizard made a face. "Oh dear, that *is* a challenge."

"*Hey*," Teddy said, with an assertiveness that Darius wasn't used to. "It was easy with the others."

The Wizard of Pride smiled at him. "I'm only joking. Your request is the easiest request. You've known it all along and you just didn't realize it." He pulled a red heart pin out of his back pocket and pinned it to Teddy's shirt. "You have to start trusting yourself and you have to start believing in who you are. You were born beautiful and good, and you have so much heart. It doesn't matter what anyone else says. That's their problem, not yours. There's nothing wrong with you as you are right now, but you have to realize this and learn to love yourself for who you are. You don't want to change. You don't want to become someone you're not. You're a kind human being with nothing but love in your heart and you have to learn how to recognize this and own it. Being a real man has nothing to do with gestures or how someone speaks. You, my friend, are a real man."

Teddy looked down at the pin on his chest and smiled. "Do you really think so?"

Darius threw his arms around Teddy and hugged

him tightly. "Of course. We all think so. And frankly, we could all learn how to do this a little better. It's not just your problem, Teddy. All men like us feel the same way. We just have to think differently, and we have to let go of all the self-loathing and guilt and shame that we've been taught to believe. There is nothing wrong with us, and there never was anything wrong with us."

After they all congratulated themselves, they hugged and everyone grew more animated. Darius was so thrilled they'd all been granted their requests he completely forgot about his own request. Then Teddy said, "Hey, what about Darius."

The Wizard of Pride rubbed his chin and Darius looked down at the pink high heels. "I don't think the Wizard can do anything for me now. I'm afraid I'll never see Uranus again, Teddy." He knew his request wasn't emotional, and it was something that couldn't be repaired by his thoughts or his wishes. What he needed was more practical and the Wizard of Pride didn't seem very magical and mystical to him any longer.

While the others shook their heads, The Wizard lifted his head and said, "Don't underestimate me, Darius. There's only one way to give you what you want and I'll have to do it myself."

"You can help me get to Uranus?" Darius asked.

"Why of course I can," said the Wizard. "I'm from Kansas myself, and I know how to get back there. I'll take you there myself."

"You know how to do that?" Darius asked. Although he felt a strong connection and attraction to the Wizard of Pride, he still wasn't convinced he was a real Wizard.

The Wizard ignored his question and turned and

walked toward the exit. "We have plans to make, big plans. We'll make this a huge celebration and invite everyone in Rainbow City to attend. There will be music and dancing and male strippers on poles. We'll have escargot, and champagne, and the best caviar there is."

"And cheese," said Teddy. He smiled at Darius. "I just *love* my cheese."

"Yes, and cheese," said the Wizard.

Darius followed him toward the exit and said, "Male strippers on poles?"

The Wizard of Pride turned and smiled. "Oh yes, there will definitely be male strippers on poles. Everything about this celebration will be wonderful, happy, and gay, and no one will ever forget it."

As they stood there in the doorway and the others watched from a distance, the Wizard of Pride reached out and put his arms around Darius. He held him tightly and gazed into his eyes. Neither one of them said a word, but Darius' heart was beating so fast by then he knew this would be a celebration he would never forget.

Chapter Seventeen

They were all so jaded from their grueling ordeal at the Wicked Fairy's castle that Strong Man kept yawning and Teddy complained about his feet hurting. Even Butch admitted that he could use a nap, so the Wizard of Pride made a public announcement that day and he declared it a national day of rest in Rainbow City. Then he sent Strong Man, Teddy, Butch and even Sparky off to a spa where they would be pampered and refreshed and groomed in preparation of the huge going away celebration the next morning.

As they all trailed off into the heart of Rainbow City again, Darius smiled at the Wizard of Pride and said, "You certainly did something wonderful for each one of them. I've never seen them so happy. You're a very wise and knowing Wizard. I'm sorry I doubted you."

The Wizard just shrugged. "I didn't do anything more than reassure them with facts they already knew about themselves. I think they'll all be fine now."

Darius nodded. "I think so, too. Now if you can only get me back to Uranus that would be wonderful. I know that's a much more difficult request and I don't want to pressure you."

The Wizard looked directly into his eyes. "You

y

160

should relax now, too. Would you like to return to the football players' locker room and see the guys again?"

"Not really," Darius said. "That kind of thing is fun for the moment, and it's a novelty that I really did enjoy at the time. But it's not the kind of thing I like to make a habit of doing. The only thing I ever wanted was to find a real man to love and be with for the rest of my life."

The Wizard of Pride smiled wider. "We could spend some time together. I would really like that."

Darius looked up at him and nodded fast. "Oh, I would love that." There was something about this man who referred to himself as the Wizard of Pride that Darius found hard to resist. He appeared strong, and yet he was vulnerable and delicate. He exuded self-confidence, and yet underneath he seemed fragile and cautious. Darius felt a strong attraction to him, and it wasn't just his dark, masculine good looks either. It was a deeper connection that Darius couldn't figure out no matter how hard he tried. It was as though they'd already been together.

The Wizard of Pride placed his palm on Darius' back and led him to another section of the Rainbow City that he referred to as his private palace, and Darius followed without any hesitation. "It's really not a palace," the Wizard said. "It's more like a penthouse apartment with a grand title. I landed here in the Land of Pride just like you and they made me the honorary Wizard of Pride. Half the time I don't know what the hell I'm doing but they seem to trust me and of course I would never do anything to harm them. This is a good place."

Darius just listened to him without saying a word.

After a short walk through a more isolated part of the city, they reached a tall narrow set of gilded doors. The Wizard opened one door and gestured for Darius to enter first, and then he followed Darius into a beautiful, simple group of rooms. There wasn't much furniture, but everything that was there appeared to be new and shiny and futuristic. The walls and floor were white marble, the trim was all black, and there were walls of glass that overlooked the greenest countryside Darius had ever seen.

Darius walked over to a wall of glass not far from a large white platform bed and said, "This is amazing. It feels as though I'm looking into a French impressionist painting." He'd read about this kind of art at the Uranus public library and he'd fallen in love with the style. Everything about Rainbow City and the Land of Pride seemed too good to be true.

The Wizard stepped up behind him and said, "It is magnificent, isn't it?"

"Oh yes," Darius said. "And I can't thank you enough for helping us all this way." His heart was beating faster and he wanted to reach out and caress the Wizard's face but he didn't want to appear too aggressive and he didn't want to exploit the Wizard's kindness. But most of all, he didn't want the Wizard to think he was a slut.

"You don't have to thank me," the Wizard said. "I'm looking forward to taking you back home to Uranus. I'm not from Rainbow City either and it's time for me to go home again, too. I landed here by accident and it's been wonderful, but it's time. I'm not the Wizard of anything, at least not by nature. I'm just a regular guy from Kansas who everyone knows as KT."

"Is your name KT?" Darius asked. "What does it stand for?" He figured they were initials.

"That's it," KT said. "That's the only name I ever had, KT Brown. My mother wasn't fond of traditional names, and she always liked shortcuts, so she simply decided to call me KT and be done with it."

Darius hesitated for a second, but then he reached out and caressed KT's arm. "I like it, KT. It's simple, but strong, and it suits you well."

"You're very kind," KT said.

"I mean it." He wanted to rip KT's clothes right off his body, but he didn't dare. He wanted KT to make the first move. "Can I ask you a question?"

"Sure."

"Do you think I'm a slut?"

KT sent him a smile and laughed. "Of course not. I think you're adorable. I think everything about you is adorable. You're just a free spirit who loves life. Don't ever let anyone fault you for that. People will try, but don't you let them."

"Do you really think so?"

KT nodded.

Darius wanted him so much by then he began to perspire. He turned and looked into KT's eyes and they exchanged a long glance. A minute later, they were locked in a tight embrace, they were kissing, and KT was guiding him toward the large white bed. They kissed for a few more minutes at the foot of the bed, and then they both stripped off their clothes and jumped into bed so fast Darius accidentally hit KT in the jaw with his elbow.

"I'm so sorry," Darius said. He kissed his jaw gently.

KT grabbed him by the shoulders, forced him onto his back, and climbed on top of him. "I'm fine. Don't you worry about me."

"I wish I could remove these pink high heels," Darius said. "Sometimes, like right now, I feel silly in them."

"I like them," KT said. "There's no reason to feel awkward with me, especially in Rainbow City. There are no gender boundaries here."

Darius spread his legs wider and they started kissing again. He lifted his legs higher and KT kissed him harder. The love they made that afternoon was very different and Darius couldn't figure out why it was different. It was familiar, as if they'd already made love, and yet Darius knew that had to be impossible. For one thing, Darius still wasn't completely sure about anything with regard to the Land of Pride and Rainbow City. It all seemed too good to be true, and after a lifetime of disappointment and regret he'd learned to proceed with a great deal of caution. The only thing Darius knew for certain was that he was in the middle of an unforgettable moment that he knew would one day become a blessed memory.

After they kissed for a while in the missionary position, which would have been fine with Darius if that's all they'd done, KT did something to Darius that no man had ever done. He seemed to care about pleasing Darius as much as Darius cared about pleasing him. And when he turned Darius over and he buried his face between Darius' legs and began to rim his anus, Darius lifted his head and let out a soft moan that left him breathless.

No man had ever done this to Darius and the

pleasure he experienced at that moment created a stir within his body that left him begging for more. The more KT licked and poked with his tongue the wider Darius spread his legs. There wasn't much verbal interaction, and Darius didn't exaggerate when he moaned. They seemed to follow an unplanned pattern, as if each one of them knew what the other expected and needed without having to ask.

KT seemed to know Darius enjoyed getting slapped on the bottom in a playful, harmless way. He seemed to know that it made Darius' heart pound faster when he rubbed his beard into his bottom. KT licked, he bit, he groped, and he slapped Darius on the ass so much that when it was time for him to climb onto Darius' back and enter him, Darius didn't even need lubrication. He was so eager for KT to enter his body he arched his back and started sucking KT's fingers in a way that would have appeared vulgar and idiotic under any other circumstances. Sometimes, though not always, when Darius was alone after he'd had sex with a man, he laughed and thought about some of the more ridiculous things he'd done. While he'd been performing these sexual acts, it wasn't funny at all. But afterward he usually took pleasure in knowing that certain sexual acts did, in fact, tend to be amusing under normal circumstances.

Although Darius never saw anything wrong with a little dirty talk, he also knew that the best lovers usually know what to do without having to be told. It's instinctive, and it's raw, and that's what KT did to him that afternoon. He shoved the head of his erection into Darius' anus, entered him, and slid all the way to the bottom with one quick move. There was nothing

Ryan Field

uncomfortable about it, and in the same respect nothing seemed to have been planned. It was that rare kind of natural experience that only two lovers share once or twice in a lifetime if they are lucky.

Darius moaned softly and nodded as KT went deeper. Then he remained still for a moment and he kissed the back of Darius' neck. When he finally began to move his pelvis and slid in and out of Darius, it was hard for Darius to focus on anything but the man who was inside him. This was better than being with any of the farm hands he'd known, it was better than being with any of the friends he'd made on this trip to the Land of Pride. Darius felt as if he'd found something unique that afternoon with KT and he knew it was because he had feelings for him. He still didn't know if he could call it love, because he wasn't certain at that point he was allowed to love another man this way. He'd always been taught to believe this kind of love was reserved for men and women, not for two men. But it felt like love, and it made him feel thrilled to be alive.

KT made love to Darius on his back, on his side, on his knees from behind, and then they finally returned to the missionary position with Darius flat on his back again. This intense non-stop fucking lasted for so long, and he kept Darius on the edge of climax for so long, Darius wondered where KT found all this stamina. With other men Darius didn't mind if it happened fast, but with KT he didn't want it to end, not ever.

On that afternoon, Darius came with KT's hand pressed to his throat, and as Darius reached his climax, KT came inside him. KT remained still for a moment, with his hand still pressed against Darius' throat and not a word spoken. When he recovered he leaned over, gently kissed Darius on the lips, and slowly rested on top of Darius until they both went flaccid.

When Darius finally climbed out of bed, he was alone in the room. KT had gone off somewhere to check on the preparations for the going away event in the morning. He seemed so animated as he kissed Darius goodbye and promised it would be an event Darius would never forget. But Darius had a feeling he was missing something important and he couldn't quite put his finger on what exactly it was. Before he put on his clothes, he crossed to a wall of glass and glanced out at the gardens surrounding the Rainbow City and wondered if he would ever see his loved ones again.

Chapter Eighteen

Early the next morning, KT climbed off Darius and ran to a chair on the other side of the room to put on his clothes. Darius lifted his head from the pillow, rubbed his eyes so he could focus, and watched KT fumble as he tried to put on his pants. They'd made love three more times that night and Darius had slept so well after the third time he couldn't believe it was already morning. He laughed and said, "You're in such a rush you didn't even put on your underwear."

KT pulled up his zipper and sent him a smile. "I don't want to waste a moment. The celebration has already begun and we're on our way back to Kansas. I'll buy new underwear when I'm home. You'd better get ready, too. The magic carpet leaves at noon, sharp."

"I'll be up in a moment," Darius said. He'd slept so well and felt so relaxed he hated getting out of bed. He was laying there naked, wearing nothing but the glittery pink high heels. Darius wouldn't have minded if KT climbed back into bed just one last time and made love to him.

He knew that wasn't going to happen. KT finished dressing fast and turned on the way to the bedroom door. "I'll see you in a few minutes. Don't take too long."

Darius lifted his leg and waved at him with his foot. "I'll be there in a few minutes. I promise."

After KT left, Darius started to think about Uranus and Etienne. He missed her so much he climbed out of bed and started getting dressed, too. He missed the farm, he missed his uncle, and he even missed the farm hands he used to sneak around with in the barn. He found it ironic that he had to lose almost everything to realize how much he really did love his own life. The only problem was that he'd always been so torn because of who he was. In the Land of Pride he could be free and open about his attraction to men. He didn't have to hide and he didn't have to pretend anything here. Even though he wasn't the type of man who would normally walk around in Uranus in pink glittery high heels i n broad daylight, it was nice to know that there was a place like Pride where things like this didn't matter. Everyone in Pride was equal and free and no one was ever targeted or bullied for being slightly different.

Darius would miss the feeling of safety the most in the Land of Pride. He also knew he had to go home, and maybe he could help fight to make a difference back there. Maybe someday in the future people like him who were not mainstream would find their own sense of Pride and they could live the lives they were meant to live. He vowed that morning that if he ever did get back to Uranus he would try to make a difference.

On his way out the door, he checked the bedroom mirror to make sure his collar was even. He straightened his tuxedo jacket and adjusted his short pants. As he turned and opened the door, he now felt as though he had to go home. He wasn't quite sure why he felt this strong need. He just knew he had to get back there.

When he entered the main square centered in the middle of Rainbow City, he saw people dancing and laughing and eating the most wonderful foods. This wasn't the kind of breakfast celebration he would have seen in Uranus. There was a life-sized statue of a naked cowboy as a fountain, standing proud, strong, and, most importantly, hard in all its glory. But this wasn't just any decorative fountain. This one had thick creamy white chocolate flowing from the cowboy's penis and people were standing in line to taste it. There was a table layered with the finest French pastries, another table with puddings and cakes and pies, and yet another large table where colorfully dressed people stood in line waiting to sample every flavor of ice cream that had ever been created.

As he crossed in front of a group of gorgeous naked men singing Christmas songs, KT called out his name and said, "Get over here this instant. There's been a change of plans. We're not leaving at noon. We have to leave right now. Hurry up."

Darius glanced to his left and spotted KT standing on a platform in the middle of the square, with Strong Man, Butch and Teddy. When he saw Sparky, he waved in their direction and said, "Wait for me. Don't leave without me."

He ran as fast as he could in glittery pink high heels. By the time he reached the platform he was so out of breath he fumbled for words. He bent down and hugged Sparky, and then he glanced up at KT and asked, "What's happened? Why are we in a hurry?"

KT was standing on the magic carpet and it

seemed to be moving back and forth a little. There were four men from town holding down each corner. "The magic carpet is ready to leave now. I have no control over that. We either leave now, or it will leave without us."

"Ah well, I'm glad I got here in time," Darius said. He grabbed Sparky by the collar and guided him to the magic carpet where they both stood beside KT.

When Darius was safely on the carpet beside him, KT lifted his head and said, "I'll have to make this fast. Please listen everyone. There's not much time."

The crowd turned to face him, all the music and dancing stopped, and everyone waited for him to speak. He cleared his throat and said, "I have no idea how long I'll be gone, or if I will ever return to the Land of Pride so by the power invested in me I hereby declare Teddy the brand new official Wizard of Pride."

Teddy's face lit up and he squared his back. "I'm the new Wizard? I've always wanted to be a queen, but I'm okay with Wizard. Do I get to wear a tiara?"

KT smiled. "Honey, you can wear anything you want. You can be the queen or the wizard. This is your show now."

Darius turned and reached out to hug Teddy, and then he hugged them all and said, "Oh, I'll miss all of you so much. You've been the most wonderful friends a guy like me could ever have. I don't know what I'll do without you."

Teddy winked and said, "You'll be fine. Sluts always bounce back fast. But I'll miss you just as much. And you will always be welcome here in Pride."

Butch smiled and patted Darius on the bottom

one last time. "You're a pro, baby. Be good to yourself."

Then Strong Man leaned over and kissed Darius. "You're the best, and don't ever let anyone tell you that you're not."

Darius felt a sting in his eye and he turned fast so no one would see him crying. He could feel the magic carpet moving beneath his feet and he knew they were about to take off. However, as he turned he saw Sparky spotting a pink and purple squirrel in one of the cotton candy trees in the square and he jumped off the carpet to chase it. When he lunged for the squirrel, he knocked over one of the men who'd been holding the carpet in place. Of course Darius ran after Sparky. He wasn't going to leave without him. He grabbed Sparky's collar before he had a chance to jump off the platform but when he spun around to run back to the magic carpet it was already in mid-air.

Darius threw his arms up and said, "Wait, please. You can't leave without me."

KT was already floating toward the clouds. He looked back and shrugged. "I can't help it. It's too late. I wish you luck, Darius. Be safe."

As KT's voice trailed off he glanced down at the people in town and waved goodbye. Darius watched him floating into the sky and he felt a thump in his stomach that made him want to cry. Now he knew he'd never return to Uranus or to the people he loved. He'd never see the farm again and he'd never get a chance to be truthful with Etienne.

He turned toward the others and reached for Butch's arm. "That's it. I'll never see Uranus again."

"If it helps, I'm kind of glad you're not going.

You're much better off here in the Land of Pride with people like you. You should be with people who are just like you, not back in Uranus where everyone will judge you and ridicule you."

"Thank you," Darius said. "I know you mean that with love, but this means I'm never going to see the people I love ever again, especially Etienne."

Then Teddy pointed to the sky and said, "Look. I can't believe it."

As they all turned and glanced toward where Teddy was pointing, a pink puff of cloud appeared in the distance. It floated toward them and Strong Man said, "You're going to be fine now, Darius. I just know it."

The pink cloud puff landed in the same spot where the magic carpet had been and Miss Glitz, the Good Fairy, stepped out and sent them all a warm smile. She was wearing a pink puffy gown, the diamond tiara, and the same magnificent diamond earrings that resembled crystal chandeliers. She glided toward where Darius was standing with the others and waved her long French tipped manicure gently.

When Miss Glitz was standing in front of them, smiling at Darius, Teddy curtsied and Darius said, "I need your help. If you can't help me no one can."

Miss Glitz double snapped Darius and put her hand on her hip. "Nonsense, doll. You don't need a drag queen to help you. Think about it. Sluts always bounce back."

Teddy laughed.

Darius shrugged and spread his arms out wide. "That's what Teddy said."

"He's right, doll," said Miss Glitz. "You're

wearing the magic high heels. You've always been able to get back home."

Butch made a face and groaned. "You could have told him, you know."

Miss Glitz shot him a look and lifted one eyebrow. "I'm the Good Fairy. I don't *have* to do anything, doll."

Darius felt his heart begin to race. "I don't understand."

"You should by now," Miss Glitz said. "You've learned a great deal in the Land of Pride."

Strong Man smiled. "I know I've learned a lot since I've been here. Think about it, Darius. Think about it hard."

Darius lowered his head and concentrated. When he'd arrived in the Land of Pride he'd been saturated in fear and shame. When Agnes McCain threatened to expose him to everyone, she had terrified him to the point of exhaustion and he didn't know where to turn. Running away seemed to be the only real option at the time. Leaving everyone and everything he'd ever loved seemed to be the only choice he had. However, he felt different now. He didn't feel like running anymore. He wasn't ashamed of himself, he wasn't a slut, and he'd done nothing wrong. He couldn't help it if he'd been born a certain way, and being in the Land of Pride had helped him realize that he had nothing to fear anymore. He could face everyone and be honest and open about who he was and the kind of life he wanted to live. Of course he knew he would always have to be discreet in his world, but at least he could be honest with Etienne and the rest of the people he loved.

He turned toward Miss Glitz and said, "I'm okay. There's nothing wrong with me. There never was anything wrong with me in the first place. I can go back home and face everyone with my head high and my heart full. And if they don't accept me, and they don't want me for who I am, at least I tried. I was honest with them and with myself."

"That's it, doll," Miss Glitz said. "But you had to figure that out for yourself. All people like us have to figure that out for ourselves otherwise it won't work. But there is one thing I can tell you, and I have never seen it fail. Once we do figure this out, and we are honest and open about who we are, we can begin to finally love ourselves. And I have never once seen anyone regret doing that. Not once."

"I'm ready now," Darius said. He reached down to pet Sparky. "We're both ready."

After he gave all the guys one last goodbye kiss, he wiped a tear from his eye and turned to face Miss Glitz. She waved her long fingernails over his head and said, "Close your eyes and repeat this over and over: the truth will set me free."

When he closed his eyes, he said, "The truth will set me free. The truth will set me free. The truth will set me free…" As Darius repeated it, he felt himself drifting away from Miss Glitz, these wonderful men who had become his good friends, and from the Land of Pride. He knew that once the journey began he couldn't stop drifting away, because this was his destiny and he was returning to where he belonged. He was tired of running and tired of hating himself. And whether or not his life in Uranus would get better or worse, he still had to return and be the man he'd always dreamed he could be.

Chapter Nineteen

When Darius opened his eyes and found that he was back in Uranus in his own bed at the farm, he blinked a few times and looked around to make sure it was real. So much had happened he wasn't sure about anything. The room appeared to be the same. His childhood bed was still up against the wall with the faded old floral wallpaper, the rickety old dresser that had chipped white paint was still on the other wall, and his extra pair of overalls were still hanging on a hook on the back of his crooked bedroom door. From what he could see, the house hadn't been uprooted and it hadn't flown into the middle of the twister. But more than that, the house hadn't fallen on a wicked fairy. He felt so confused he blinked again just to make sure he wasn't dreaming that he was home.

At the foot of his bed he heard a familiar voice. "Look, Nicola. He's awake." It was Etienne and she was standing at the foot of the bed next to Nicola, with her hands clasped together and a relieved expression on her face.

"Well yes, he is awake," said Nicola, with a huge smile. He sent Darius a glance. "We've been worried about you, young man. Very worried, indeed."

Sparky barked and Darius looked down and saw

him resting on the floor beside his bed. Darius looked at his aunt and uncle and said, "Etienne, you're here. You're both here. I can't believe I made it back home. I never thought I'd see you two again. You have no idea where I've been and what I've gone through." He pulled the covers back, looked down at his feet, and noticed that the glittery pink high heels were gone, and he was wearing his overalls again.

"You just rest for a while," Etienne said. "You got caught up in the storm and you've been sleeping for a while. You need rest."

"Oh, but I was gone for days," Darius said. "You have no idea where I've been. I went to this place called Pride, and then…"

In the middle of his sentence, Jasper walked into the bedroom with a serious look and asked, "How is he?"

Nicola smiled. "He's just fine now. He'll be okay."

Jasper looked down at Darius and sighed. "Well that's a relief. I've been so worried. I'd hate to see anything happen to him. He's a special guy." Then he sent Darius a wink, and he wasn't stuttering.

Eddie and Tommy entered the room and they stepped up behind Jasper. "It's so good to see him awake, " Eddie said.

"Is he going to be okay?" Tommy asked.

Etienne smiled. "He's going to be just fine. All he needs is a little rest and he'll be back to normal before this day is over."

Darius glanced up wide-eyed as they all stood over him. He'd been sleeping with all of them separately for a while and he'd never had them in his bedroom all at the same time. They were all smiling and offering him words of encouragement and he couldn't stop thinking about the Land of Pride and the wonderful, magnificent Rainbow City. With the exception of Etienne and Nicola, they'd all been there, but not exactly as they were right now, and he found it so difficult to process his head began to pound.

He started talking about where he'd been, and telling them about Teddy, Strong Man and Butch. When he mentioned the Wizard of Pride and the Wicked Fairy, Etienne took his hand in hers and said, "You'll be fine, dear. You're just a little confused right now. That was a serious blow to your head and you just need to settle down."

He glanced around the room. "No one believes me. I swear it really happened."

Sparky jumped up on his bed and this time Etienne didn't chase him off. She shook her head and said, "You rest now, dear. We'll leave you alone with Sparky and I'll be back to check on you."

When she reached for his hand this time, Darius felt a wave of relief. He smiled and nodded. "I'm okay now. It doesn't matter where I went or what happened, because now I'm home and I'm never going to leave again. At least I'm never going to leave again if you still want me around. I have a few things to talk to you about, and it's not going to be easy." He wanted to talk to them before Agnes McCain had a chance to tell them what she'd seen in the barn.

"Of course we still want you around," Nicola said.

Etienne smiled. "There is nothing on Earth you could say or do to make us not want you around,

Darius. Why would you even think that? I may not have given birth to you, but you're my son nonetheless and nothing will ever change that. I love you."

Etienne released his hand and they all turned toward the door. On her way out she sent him a backward glance and said, "You rest now. I'll be back."

When they were all gone, he set his head back on the pillow and closed his eyes. He didn't keep them closed for long, though, because a voice from the open window above his bed said, "Hey, how's it going. I've been worried sick over you."

Darius sat up fast and turned. He saw Kit standing in the open window and he got up on his knees to hug him. He threw his arms around him and said, "I'm so glad to see you. You were there, too. You were the Wizard of Pride."

Kit hugged him tighter and laughed. "I have no idea what you're talking about, but for a hug like this. I'll agree to anything." Then he reached down and patted Darius on the bottom a few times.

"Are *you* okay?" Darius asked. The last thing he remembered was making love to Kit and then running back to the farm.

"I'm just fine," Kit said. "I'm the one who found you. After you left, I started to worry about you getting home safely so I set out to make sure you were okay. Sure enough, I found you passed out on the bed covered with wood and some other debris. I pulled everything off you and I stayed with you until everyone else came up from the storm cellar."

Darius tilted his head. "You did that for me? You came to my rescue that way. You're my hero."

"Of course I did," he said, and then he kissed him on the lips a few times. "I know this sounds crazy, and maybe I shouldn't say it, but I love you. I knew I loved you the moment I saw you. When I thought you'd been hurt, it gutted me. I should never have let you leave that way. I should have insisted you stay with me until the storm was over."

Darius held him tighter. "I love you, too, Kit. I know we haven't known each other very long, but I've never felt this way before. I didn't even know two men could feel this way about each other. I always thought it had to be about sex, and that it had to be a big secret. But this is different. I love you in a different way and I never want to be without you again."

"Well I'm not going anywhere, Darius," Kit said. "I plan to be in Uranus for a long, long time. I think that coming to this town to start my practice was meant to be."

Then they kissed again, and when they stopped kissing the bedroom door opened and Etienne charged into the room with another quilt. Although they weren't doing anything sexual, Darius still had his palms pressed to Kit's chest and he pulled them back fast. He knew she hadn't seen him kissing Kit, but she had seen him touching him in a questionable way.

Etienne stopped and stood still in the doorway. "I'm sorry," she said. "I should have knocked first." She nodded at Kit and said, "This nice young doctor is the one who pulled the boards off you and he stayed with you until we came up from the cellar. He might have saved your life."

"Yes, he just told me," Darius said. Even though her expression remained stoic, he knew she was wondering why he'd been touching Kit that way. He was tired of hiding it, and he was tired of pretending to be someone he wasn't. He didn't want to spend the rest of his life fearing people like Agnes McCain. He looked into Etienne's eyes and said, "There's something I have to tell you, Etienne. You're not going to like it, but I have to tell you anyway."

Kit took a step back and said, "I should leave and let you talk. I'll come back later to check on you."

"No, please stay, Kit," Darius said. "I want you here."

Then he glanced at Etienne and said, "Something happened at the Riggleby Farm, and it involved Agnes McCain, and I have to tell you about it. I can't let it wait it's too important."

Etienne took a deep breath and shrugged. "You don't have to tell me about Agnes McCain. I've already spoken with her. I've taken care of her. You'll never have to worry about her again."

"You have?"

Etienne nodded. "She came here after the storm looking for Sparky and she told me a few things about you, and then I told *her* a few things. This is a small town and I know a few secrets about Agnes McCain that no one else knows. She didn't think I'm tough enough to stand up to her, but I am. So you see, you have nothing to worry about. Agnes McCain will not bother you ever again."

Darius tilted his head and said, "I'm not sure I understand." He wasn't curious about Agnes McCain or her secrets. He was more curious about what Etienne had heard about him.

Etienne looked up at Kit, and then she looked at

Darius. "When you were a child, Darius, you used to walk around in these pink high heels I had in the back of my closet. They were much too high and showy and I never wore them. But you loved them. You were so adorable I couldn't stop you, and neither could Nicola." She took a step closer and reached for his hand. "I know about you, Darius. I've always known about you."

"You have?"

She nodded. "I've known since you were about three years old. And I love you just as much now as I ever did. I can't tell you it's ever going to be easy. I wish I could tell you that. But you're strong, and you've got a good strong man in Kit. What more could I ask for?"

Kit smiled and nodded at her. "Thank you."

Darius felt a sting in his eye. He jumped out of bed, ran to her, and hugged her so tightly they fell back into the dresser. "I love you so much, Etienne."

She patted him on the back and took a step back. "I know that, too," she said. "Now get back into the bed and get some rest. This has been a long day. I'll leave you alone with Kit for a moment, but I want you to rest."

"I won't stay for long," Kit said.

Before she left, Darius had to know one more thing. "Did Agnes mention anyone else? Or did she just mention me?" He wanted to know if Jasper, Eddie and Tommy were safe from being exposed. He was worried about them because they weren't like him. They wanted their lives to move in a more traditional way and he didn't want to see them get hurt. Even though he didn't understand them, and he never would understand them, he knew it wasn't his choice to judge them either.

Etienne sent him a smile. "She only mentioned you, and not another name was spoken. And I can promise you she will never mention this incident again. This entire topic is over." Then she left them alone and closed the bedroom door.

He didn't ask about the secrets Etienne knew about Agnes McCain partly because it was hard for Darius to process the kind of relief he felt when Etienne told him she'd always known about him. Even though none of them went into any great lengths about his situation, and at the time there really weren't any words other than pejoratives to describe his situation, his secret was finally out in the open with the people he cared the most about. And that was all that mattered to him. He knew that in a small town in 1939 he would always have to be discreet, but he wasn't living a total lie anymore.

He turned and crossed to the window again, and he put his arms around Kit and said, "I can't believe she's always known."

"You're very lucky," Kit said. "Your aunt and uncle are special people. I like them both."

"You'll always have a home here," Darius said. "And I'll always love you."

They kissed for a few more minutes and then Kit stepped away from the window and said, "You should rest now. And that's doctor's orders. I'll be back in a few hours to check on you. We can talk more, and I'll tell you about my plans to set up a practice here in Uranus. I'd like you to be part of it, if you're willing to do that. I'll need all the help I can get. I think if we work as partners and we're discreet no one will question us. They may whisper behind our backs, but that's to be expected."

"Of course I'll help," Darius said. "I'd love that."

As Kit turned to leave, he said, "I love you. Get some rest."

Before Darius climbed back into bed he watched Kit walk away from the house, down the path that led to the barn, and back toward the old dirt road. He knew they would always have to be cautious simply because that's the way society dictated the rules, and he knew that the world was not ready for men like them yet. However, he also knew he had many things to look forward to in his future now, and support from his aunt and uncle made everything so much easier. There would always be people like Agnes McCain who were ready to judge him and tear him down, but he'd learned a few things in the Land of Pride that he would never forget. If a place like the Rainbow City could exist in his dreams, maybe someday a place like that could exist in the real world, where men like him could be proud and gay, and live open, honest lives. It was as though the universe opened up completely, and the possibilities seemed endless.

About the Author

Ryan Field is a gay fiction writer who has worked in many areas of publishing for the past 20 years. He's the author of the bestselling Virgin Billionaire series and the short story, "Down the Basement," which was included in the Lambda Award winning anthology titled *Best Gay Erotica 2009*. Though not always, he sometimes writes gay parodies of straight mainstream fiction/films in the same way straight fiction and Hollywood has been parodying gay men for years, without apology. He also writes hetero romances under pen names and has edited several short story anthologies. *Chase of a Lifetime* is his first self-published 99-cent Amazon Kindle book. It's a 60,000 word full length novel in the gay erotic romance genre.

He has a long list of publishing credits that include over 100 works of LGBT fiction, some with pen names in various sub-genres. His email is listed, and he welcomes all comments, or through email. Please check out his web site for updates because this page is not always up to date. www.ryan-field. blogspot.com You can reach at mailto:rfieldj@aol.com Follow Facebook Fan Page: Books by Ryan Field:
https://www.facebook.com/Books-by-Ryan-Field-112186572328/

Other Riverdale Avenue Books Titles
By Ryan Field You Might Enjoy

A Starr is Born

Sleepless in San Francisco

Pretty Man

A Christmas Carl

Fangsters: Clan of the Jersey Boys

Fangsters 2: Gangbang Fangsters

Valley of the Dudes

Stepbrothers in the Attic

Dancing Dirty

Other Titles by Ryan Field

Ryan Field Press Titles
A Life Filled with Awesome Love
A Regular Bud
A Sign from Heaven Above
A Young Widows Promise
All About Yves
Altered Parts
American Star
American Star II
An Officer and His Gentleman
Another Regular Bud
Baby Cakes
Big Bad And On Top
Billabong Bang
Bury it Officer
Cage James
Capping the Season
Captain Velvet's Velvet Box
Cherry Soda Cowboy
Cowboy Christmas Miracle
Cowboy Howdy
Cowboy Mike and Buddy Boy
Dancing Dirty
Dirty Little Virgin
Field of Dreams
Four Feet Under

Four Gay Weddings and a Funeral
Gay Pride and Prejudice
He's Bewitched
Hot Italian Lover
Imperfect
In Their Prime
Internal Desires
It's Nice to be Naughty
Jolly Roger
Jonah Sweet of Delancey Street
Kendle's Fire
Kevin Loves Cowboys
Meadows Are Not Forever
Missing Jackson's Hole
My Fair Laddie
New Adult Love Story
Pretty Man
Pumpkin Ravioli Boy
Ricky's Business
Rough Naked and in Love
Said With Care
Shakespeare's Lover
Sir, Yes Sir!
Skater Boy
Sleepless in San Francisco
Something for Saint Jude
Strawberries and Cream at the Plaza
Take Me Always
That Cowboy in the Window
The Arrangement
The Bachelor
The Buckhampton Country Club
The Computer Tutor Box

The Ghost and Mr. Moore
The Mile High Club
The Preacher's Husband
The Sheriff And The Outlaw
The Way We Almost Were
The Women Who Love To Love Gay Romance
Too Hard To Handle
Unabated
Uncertainty
Unmentionable: The Men Who Loved on the Titanic
Vance's Flame
Whatever Dude
When A Man Loves A Man
When Harry Met Sal
With this Cowboy I Love so Freely
You Missed a Spot Big Guy
Young Doughy Joey
Young Hung and Hitched

Bad Boy Billionaire Series
Cowboy in Love
Palm Beach Sex Scandal
Silicon Valley Sex Scandal
Small Town Romance Writer
The Actor Learning to Love
The Arrangement
The Ivy League Rake
The Vegas Shark
The Wall Street Shark

Chase Series
Chase of a Christmas Dream
Chase of a Dream - Abridged
Chase of a Dream - Unabridged
Chase of a Holy Ghost
Chase of a Lifetime
Chase of an Adventure: Fifty Shades of Gay

Down The Basement Series:
Down the Basement
Down the Basement II: Santa Saturday

Second Chance Series
Second Chance
Second Chance: His Only Choice
Second Chance: The Littlest Christmas Tree
Second Chance: The Sweetest Apple

The Rainbow Detective Agency Series
The Rainbow Detective Agency — Book 1
The Rainbow Detective Agency:
L'oumo Magico - Book 2
The Rainbow Detective Agency:
The Guy With Two Penises - Book 3
The Rainbow Detective Agency: On Fleek — Book 4
The Rainbow Detective Agency: Box Set —
Books 1-4 — Book 5
The Rainbow Detective Agency:
The Scottish Duke — Book 6
The Rainbow Detective Agency:
The Wedding — Book 7

The Rainbow Detective Agency:
Saying Goodbye — Book 8
The Rainbow Detective Agency:
Rancho Mirage — Book 9

The Virgin Billionaire Series
The Virgin Billionaire
The Virgin Billionaire and the Evil Twin
The Virgin Billionaire: Revenge
The Virgin Billionaire's Dream House
The Virgin Billionaire's Hot Amish Escapade
The Virgin Billionaire's Little Angel
The Virgin Billionaire's Reversal of Fortune
The Virgin Billionaire's Secret Baby
The Virgin Billionaire's Sexcellent Adventure
The Virgin Billionaire's Wedding

www.ingramcontent.com/pod-product-compliance
Lightning Source LLC
Chambersburg PA
CBHW071434260626
47170CB00008B/2719